SMOKING

Other books in the Introducing Issues
with Opposing Viewpoints series:

INTRODUCING
ISSUES
WITH

OPPOSING VIEWPOINTS®

SMOKING

Lauri S. Friedman, *Book Editor*

Bruce Glassman, *Vice President*
Bonnie Szumski, *Publisher, Series Editor*
Helen Cothran, *Managing Editor*

OPPOSING
VIEWPOINTS®
SERIES

GREENHAVEN PRESS
An imprint of Thomson Gale, a part of The Thomson Corporation

THOMSON
—★—™
GALE

Detroit • New York • San Francisco • San Diego • New Haven, Conn. • Waterville, Maine • London • Munich

THOMSON

⭑ ™

GALE

LIBRARY OF CONGRESS CATALOGING-IN-PUBLICATION DATA

Smoking / Lauri S. Friedman, book editor.
  p. cm. — (Introducing issues with opposing viewpoints)
  Includes bibliographical references and index.
  ISBN 0-7377-3342-X (lib. : alk. paper)
  1. Tobacco habit—United States. 2. Smoking—United States—Prevention.
3. Smoking—Health aspects—United States. 4. Smoking—Economic aspects—
United States. I. Friedman, Lauri S. II. Series.
    HV5760.S664 2006
    362.29'6—dc22

                                                    2005046140

CONTENTS

I
ndulging in a wide spectrum of ideas, beliefs, and perspectives is a critical cornerstone of democracy. After all, it is often debates over differences of opinion, such as whether to legalize abortion, how to treat prisoners, or when to enact the death penalty, that shape our society and drive it forward. Such diversity of thought is frequently regarded as the hallmark of a healthy and civilized culture. As the Reverend Clifford Schutjer of the First Congregational Church in Mansfield, Ohio, declared in a 2001 sermon, "Surrounding oneself with only like-minded people, restricting what we listen to or read only to what we find agreeable is irresponsible. Refusing to entertain doubts once we make up our minds is a subtle but deadly form of arrogance." With this advice in mind, Introducing Issues with Opposing Viewpoints books aim to open readers' minds to the critically divergent views that comprise our world's most important debates.

Introducing Issues with Opposing Viewpoints simplifies for students the enormous and often overwhelming mass of material now available via print and electronic media. Collected in every volume is an array of opinions that captures the essence of a particular controversy or topic. Introducing Issues with Opposing Viewpoints books embody the spirit of nineteenth-century journalist Charles A. Dana's axiom: "Fight for your opinions, but do not believe that they contain the whole truth, or the only truth." Absorbing such contrasting opinions teaches students to analyze the strength of an argument and compare it to its opposition. From this process readers can inform and strengthen their own opinions, or be exposed to new information that will change their minds. Introducing Issues with Opposing Viewpoints is a mosaic of different voices. The authors are statesmen, pundits, academics, journalists, corporations, and ordinary people who have felt compelled to share their experiences and ideas in a public forum. Their words have been collected from newspapers, journals, books, speeches, interviews, and the Internet, the fastest growing body of opinionated material in the world.

Introducing Issues with Opposing Viewpoints shares many of the well-known features of its critically acclaimed parent series, Opposing Viewpoints. The articles are presented in a pro/con format, allowing readers to absorb divergent perspectives side by side. Active reading questions preface each viewpoint, requiring the student to approach the material thoughtfully and carefully. Useful charts, graphs, and cartoons supplement each article. A thorough introduction provides readers with crucial background on an issue. An annotated bibliography points the reader toward articles, books, and Web sites that contain additional information on the topic. An appendix of organizations to contact contains a wide variety of charities, nonprofit organizations, political groups, and private enterprises that each hold a position on the issue at hand. Finally, a comprehensive index allows readers to locate content quickly and efficiently.

Introducing Issues with Opposing Viewpoints is also significantly different from Opposing Viewpoints. As the series title implies, its presentation will help introduce students to the concept of opposing viewpoints, and learn to use this material to aid in critical writing and debate. The series' four-color, accessible format makes the books attractive and inviting to readers of all levels. In addition, each viewpoint has been carefully edited to maximize a reader's understanding of the content. Short but thorough viewpoints capture the essence of an argument. A substantial, thought-provoking essay question placed at the end of each viewpoint asks the student to further investigate the issues raised in the viewpoint, compare and contrast two authors' arguments, or consider how one might go about forming an opinion on the topic at hand. Each viewpoint contains sidebars that include at-a-glance information and handy statistics. A Facts About section located in the back of the book further supplies students with relevant facts and figures.

Following in the tradition of the Opposing Viewpoints series, Greenhaven Press continues to provide readers with invaluable exposure to the controversial issues that shape our world. As John Stuart Mill once wrote: "The only way in which a human being can make some approach to knowing the whole of a subject is by hearing what can be said about it by persons of every variety of opinion and studying all modes in which it can be looked at by every character of mind. No wise man ever acquired his wisdom in any mode but this." It is to this principle that Introducing Issues with Opposing Viewpoints books are dedicated.

"If one abolishes man's freedom to determine his own consumption, one takes all freedoms away."

—Twentieth-century economist Ludwig von Mises

"There's a very good reason why the anti-smoking movement is winning. It's not because they are health Nazis imposing their politically correct beliefs on everybody else. It's because clean air is better than dirty air and good health is better than sickness and death."

—Columnist Joel McNally

On November 23, 1998, the major American tobacco companies agreed to pay $206 billion in damages to forty-six states for the medical costs incurred by smokers as part of what became known as the Master Settlement Agreement (MSA). The MSA also required tobacco companies to finance a $1.5 billion antismoking campaign and to cease refuting evidence that smoking is harmful to human health. This landmark agreement signified a turning point in American history: For the first time, an industry was held directly responsible for damages caused to consumers of their product. Since the adoption of the MSA, those on both sides of the issue have discussed with fervor whether this settlement was an appropriate response to the issue of smoking. In the folds of this dispute lie a critical question that frequently underlines many social debates: To what extent are people responsible for their behavior?

Like other potentially harmful habits such as drinking or eating poorly, some view smoking as an inherently personal choice. After all, the health risks of smoking are widely known and have been since 1965, when Congress first required all cigarette packs to prominently display the warning, "Caution: Cigarette Smoking May Be Hazardous to Your Health." As commentator Michael Dodge has bluntly stated, "There isn't a sentient being alive who doesn't know that smoking is bad for you." Those such as Dodge believe if people want to smoke, they make this decision as informed adults and it is not society's job to "baby" them about it. Author Richard Lowry has put the issue in a

Many smokers believe the right to smoke is a guaranteed personal freedom and that antismoking legislation has no place in a democratic society.

slightly different way: "The fact is that sometimes we choose pleas-ures—smoking, drinking, gay sex—that aren't good for us. So what? . . . Are people so childish that they can't figure out for themselves whether to take 'the risk' of sharing a cigarette over a cappuccino?" Those who agree with Lowry believe it is wrong to hold the tobacco companies responsible for peoples' decision to smoke, and inappro-priate for the government to get involved in the personal decisions made by its citizenry.

Legislation to curb smoking is further interpreted by those in this camp as being an affront to personal liberty. As author James Harkin has argued, "My preference for a cigarette forms part of a class of desires that, when taken together, play an important and highly con-tested role in our understanding of freedom. . . . Smoking is a filthy habit that most of us want to give up. . . . But when this truth is employed to justify a government campaign to second-guess our desires and persuade us of the need for more responsible consumer choices, it . . . relieves the individual of responsibility for his actions and makes responsibility for those actions the stuff of good government." Indeed, many accuse those who are anti-tobacco of trying to "save people from themselves" and charge them with crossing boundaries that are integral to a democratic and free society.

On the other hand, those against tobacco argue that because smoking is such an addictive and unhealthy habit, society has an obligation to prevent as many people from smoking as it can. Though smokers may have lit their first cigarette under the assumption that it is

Dan Morales, the attorney general for Texas, holds up an oversized check. The check represents the state's share of the $206 billion American tobacco companies were ordered to pay in the MSA settlement.

their choice to smoke, in time they often find themselves battling a gripping and dangerous addiction. Many smokers, such as writer John Balzer, feel they are at the mercy of their habit: "I suck down my nicotine like any other junkie behind the bushes, full of self-loathing at my own weak stupidity." Indeed, it has been proven that the tobacco companies enhanced the amount of nicotine in a cigarette in order

Antismoking groups conduct advertising campaigns that discourage smoking, exemplified by this billboard in Little Rock, Arkansas.

to get people more addicted to their product, and pursued aggressive advertising strategies that particularly targeted women, children, and African Americans. Therefore, many often see the tobacco industry as calculating and dangerous and argue it should be held responsible for damages caused by the products it sells. Writes Balzer: "Sometimes in my dreams I can see their [the tobacco chemists'] detached, cold-blooded eyes as they rush to please their bosses . . . deliberately jacking up the addictive substance in our tobacco. People who carried on even when their own evidence showed they were wrapping bullets in paper and killing us. Then lying about it, and spending millions [on cigarette advertising] egging us on with a smile."

People of this persuasion further argue that it is perfectly appropriate for society to protect its citizenry from smoking. They point out that the government frequently shields the public from harm—from setting standards for building codes, to requiring food and drug inspections, to instituting seat belt laws—and should do no differently with smoking. Furthermore, evidence suggests that social and economic factors greatly contribute to a person's tendency to smoke, and so outside assistance may be required to prevent people from smoking or successfully help them to quit. A study by the American Legacy Foundation, for example, found that adolescents who have two parents who smoke are more than twice as likely as youths without smoking parents to become smokers. Similarly, it has been shown that those with low income and less education have an increased tendency to smoke over better-educated and wealthier people. Poor self-esteem, depression, and behavioral disorders may also contribute to a person's inclination to smoke. It is thus often suggested that the government must raise the awareness of how dangerous smoking can be and take measures to protect the at-risk sectors of the public from smoking. Who should bear responsibility for smoking and many other interesting debates are explored further in the viewpoints presented in *Introducing Issues with Opposing Viewpoints: Smoking.*

CHAPTER 1

Is Smoking a Serious Problem?

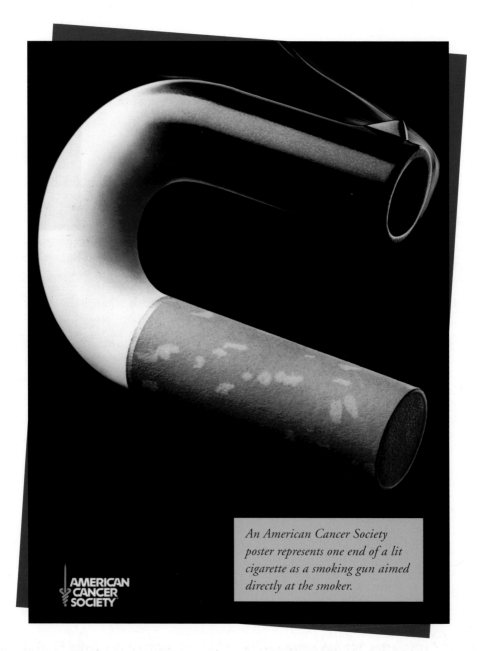

An American Cancer Society poster represents one end of a lit cigarette as a smoking gun aimed directly at the smoker.

Smoking Is Harmful to Health

James Gerstenzang

"We've known for decades that smoking is bad for your health, but this report shows that it's even worse."

James Gerstenzang is a writer for the *Los Angeles Times,* from which this viewpoint was taken. In the following article, Gerstenzang reports on the 2004 study released by the U.S. surgeon general that declared smoking is hazardous to human health, and even more so than previously thought. The study found that cigarette smoking harms almost every single organ in the human body and causes cancer in the stomach, kidney, pancreas, lung, and reproductive organs. It shortens the life-span of male and female smokers by over a decade, and multiplies the health risks of infants born to parents who smoke. Because smoking kills about 440,000 Americans per year, the surgeon general reports that it is the single greatest avoidable cause of death in the United States. Furthermore, the report contends that government is having minimal success at getting citizens to quit smoking, and poor Americans seem especially difficult to reach. The author reports that as scientific knowledge about the human body has grown, the dangers that smoking poses have become clearer and more worrisome.

AS YOU READ, CONSIDER THE FOLLOWING QUESTIONS:
  1. According to the article, do light or low-tar cigarettes have any health benefits over regular cigarettes?
  2. As suggested by people quoted in the article, what are two methods that might reduce the rate of smoking in America?
  3. According to the article, what are three illnesses linked to smoking?

Cigarette smoking harms nearly every human organ and is increasingly a habit of the poorest Americans, the federal government reported [in May 2004] in its most comprehensive look at the dangers of tobacco in three years.

Forty years after the groundbreaking surgeon general's study that alerted Americans to the cancer risk of cigarettes, the current surgeon general issued a report that linked smoking to more illnesses than previously known. [Surgeon General] Dr. Richard H. Carmona also reported that cigarettes offering lower tar and nicotine than conventional-strength cigarettes provide no clear health benefits. . . .

FAST FACT

According to the American Lung Association, there are over four thousand chemicals in tobacco, sixty-three of which cause cancer. This list includes tar, carbon monoxide, arsenic, hydrogen cyanide, acetylene, benzene, and formaldehyde.

Smoking Is More Dangerous than Previously Thought

The surgeon general's report found that as scientific knowledge has expanded, the dangers of cigarettes have grown more apparent. They go far beyond circulatory and respiratory illnesses to include risks to reproductive organs, kidneys and vision, Carmona said. His report also found that a higher number of specific types of cancer are fueled by smoking than earlier reports had stated.

To the list of illnesses and conditions linked to smoking, the surgeon general added cataracts, pneumonia, acute myeloid leukemia, abdominal aortic aneurysms, periodontitis (an inflammation of gum tissue) and cancers of the stomach, pancreas, cervix and kidney.

Nicotine is found in breast milk, Carmona said, and babies exposed to secondhand smoke are twice as likely to be victims of sudden infant death syndrome as those not exposed to it. Infants whose mothers smoked before and after birth were "at three or four times greater risk," the report said.

The Toxins Go Everywhere the Blood Flows

The report said women who smoke shorten their lives by an average of 14.5 years, and that the average loss for male smokers is 13.2 years.

"We've known for decades that smoking is bad for your health, but this report shows that it's even worse," Carmona said. "The toxins from cigarette smoke go everywhere the blood flows."

And, he added, "there is no safe cigarette, whether it is called 'light,' 'ultra-light' or any other name."

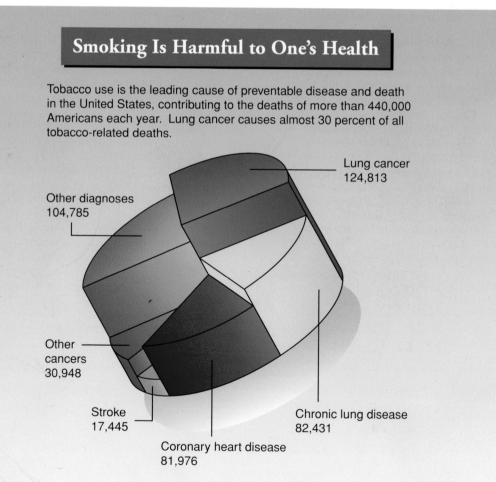

Smoking Is Harmful to One's Health

Tobacco use is the leading cause of preventable disease and death in the United States, contributing to the deaths of more than 440,000 Americans each year. Lung cancer causes almost 30 percent of all tobacco-related deaths.

Lung cancer
124,813

Other diagnoses
104,785

Other cancers
30,948

Stroke
17,445

Coronary heart disease
81,976

Chronic lung disease
82,431

Source: Centers for Disease Control and Prevention, "Targeting Tobacco Use: The Nation's Leading Cause of Death," 2004.

"Cigarette Smoking Causes Serious Diseases"

M. Cass Wheeler, president of the American Heart Assn., said the surgeon general's report should inspire stronger antitobacco action by the federal and the state governments.

"Tobacco remains the nation's most unregulated consumer product," he said, noting that Congress was considering legislation that would give the Food and Drug Administration the authority to regulate tobacco products.

On the state level, he called for increased taxes, comprehensive smoking bans and the use of money from the [1998] settlement agreement between the states and tobacco companies to fund more anti-smoking programs.

Brendan McCormick, a spokesman for cigarette maker Philip Morris USA, said, "We agree with the medical and scientific conclusions that cigarette smoking causes serious diseases in smokers, and that there is no such thing as a safe cigarette." . . .

A doctor points out a growth on the X-ray of a patient's lung that he suspects is cancerous. Lung cancer is the leading cause of death in smokers.

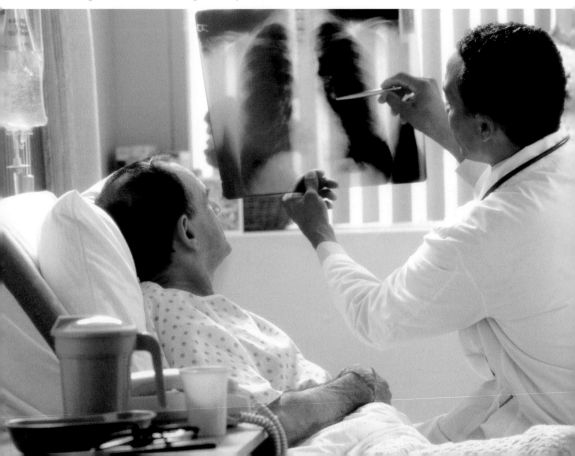

Poor Americans Need Extra Help to Quit

According to the CDC [Centers for Disease Control and Prevention], 22.2% of adult Americans living at or above the poverty level were smokers in 2002. . . .

Corinne Housten, a medical officer and epidemiologist at the CDC's office of smoking and health, said that wealthier people had greater access to programs designed to help people quit smoking and lived in a social environment in which smoking was less acceptable.

"We need to focus particular attention on these disadvantaged populations," provid-

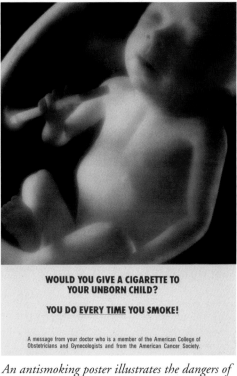

WOULD YOU GIVE A CIGARETTE TO YOUR UNBORN CHILD?

YOU DO EVERY TIME YOU SMOKE!

A message from your doctor who is a member of the American College of Obstetricians and Gynecologists and from the American Cancer Society.

An antismoking poster illustrates the dangers of smoking during pregnancy.

ing access to treatment, health insurance and local clinics providing help in breaking the smoking habit, she said.

Her views were supported by Matthew L. Myers, president of the Campaign for Tobacco-Free Kids, who called for coverage for smoking cessation programs under Medicare and Medicaid, the government healthcare programs for the elderly and the poor. He also encouraged Congress to raise the federal cigarette tax by $2 and use a portion of the proceeds for quit-smoking initiatives.

"What is most disturbing about this report is the wide gulf between the devastation caused by smoking and what our country is doing to reduce it," Myers said in a statement.

In California, the average price of a pack of cigarettes is more than $4, according to his organization.

The Greatest Avoidable Cause of Death

Although some of the previous 27 surgeon general's reports on smoking have raised the likelihood, or certainty, that smoking increased the risk of a variety of diseases, the new document goes further, stating in case after case that "the evidence is sufficient to infer a causal relationship" between smoking and a specific condition.

One by one, the reports have added to the breadth of concerns about smoking, which they count as the greatest avoidable cause of death in the United States. The executive summary of [the 2004] report said smoking causes about 440,000 deaths a year and costs approximately $157 billion in annual health-related economic losses.

The summary of the 900-page report stated: "An increasingly disturbing picture of widespread organ damage in active smokers is emerging, likely reflecting the systemic distribution of tobacco smoke components and their high level of toxicity.

"This new information should be an impetus for even more vigorous programs to reduce and prevent smoking."

EVALUATING THE AUTHORS' ARGUMENTS:

The viewpoint you just read covered the surgeon general's assessment of the health risks of cigarette smoking. In the following viewpoint, author Eric Boyd argues that these health risks are exaggerated and overstated. After reading both viewpoints, how would you assess the risks associated with cigarette smoking? Explain your answer.

VIEWPOINT 2

The Risks of Smoking Are Exaggerated

Eric Boyd

"Untold in this 'war on tobacco' is that each of the plants we consume consists of . . . thousands of chemicals, many of which are recognized poisons or suspected cancer-causing agents."

In the following viewpoint, Eric Boyd argues that the health risks associated with smoking have been overstated in an irrational and dangerous way. He suggests that while cigarettes do contain several known toxins, these chemicals are found in other items that are regarded as healthy, such as carrots, strawberries, fish, and wine. Moreover, he contends that in order for these chemicals to do serious health damage, one must smoke hundreds of thousands, even millions of cigarettes. By his account, a person would need to smoke two packs of cigarettes per day for more than sixty-eight years in order to begin approaching significant danger levels. Boyd further argues that studies citing the dangers of smoking are flawed, and the conclusions based on them by government organizations are thus invalid. He concludes by saying that overstating the risks of smoking contributes to an irrational society that will suffer a loss of personal freedom.

Eric Boyd, "The Risks of Smoking Are Greatly Exaggerated," *The Kitchener-Waterloo Record* (Ontario), November 20, 2002. Copyright © 2002 by Eric Boyd. Reproduced by permission.

Eric Boyd is a facilities manager in Canada. He has contributed to the *Kitchener-Waterloo Record*, a newspaper in the Ontario area from which this viewpoint was taken.

AS YOU READ, CONSIDER THE FOLLOWING QUESTIONS:
1. According to the author, what do tomatoes, grapefruits, and cigarettes have in common?
2. Why does the author consider the National Institutes of Health study on smoking-related deaths to be flawed?
3. According to the author, what alleged health benefits can smoking have?

Too much is made of the 4,000 chemicals in tobacco smoke. We're told these chemicals are so harmful that they are responsible for the deaths of millions worldwide. Untold in this "war on tobacco" is that each of the plants we consume consists of an equally daunting thousands of chemicals, many of which are recognized poisons or suspected cancer-causing agents.

Cayenne peppers, carrots and strawberries each contain six suspected carcinogens; onions, grapefruit and tomato each contain five—some the same as the seven suspected carcinogens found in tobacco.

High-heat cooking creates yet more dietary carcinogens from otherwise harmless chemical constituents.

> **FAST FACT**
>
> The Greeks, Japanese, and Italians are among the world's heaviest smokers, yet they have relatively high life expectancy rates and low rates of smoking-related illnesses.

Cigarette Toxins Are Found in Normal Diets

Sure, these plant chemicals are measured in infinitesimal amounts. An independent study calculated 222,000 smoking cigarettes would be needed to reach unacceptable levels of benzo(a)pyrene [a naturally occurring substance that can cause health problems]. One million smoking cigarettes would be needed to produce unacceptable levels of toluene [found in car exhaust, nail polish, and paint, among other products]. To reach these estimated danger levels, the cigarettes must be smoked simultaneously and completely in a sealed 20-square-foot room with a nine-foot ceiling.

Many other chemicals in tobacco smoke can also be found in normal diets. Smoking 3,000 packages of cigarettes would supply the same amount of arsenic as a nutritious 200 gram serving of sole [a type of fish].

Half a bottle of now healthy wine can supply 32 times the amount of lead as one pack of cigarettes. The same amount of cadmium

Surprisingly, half a bottle of wine contains many times the amount of toxic lead found in a pack of cigarettes.

obtained from smoking eight packs of cigarettes can be enjoyed in half a pound of crab.

That's one problem with the anti-smoking crusade. The risks of smoking are greatly exaggerated. So are the costs.

Anti-Smoking Studies Are Flawed

An in-depth analysis of 400,000 U.S. smoking-related deaths by National Institutes of Health mathematician Rosalind Marimont and senior fellow in constitutional studies at the Cato Institute Robert Levy identified a disturbing number of flaws in the methodology used to estimate these deaths. Incorrectly classifying some diseases as smoking-related and choosing the wrong standard of comparison each over-stated deaths by more than 65 per cent.

Failure to control for confounding variables such as diet and exercise turned estimates more into a computerized shell game than reliable estimates of deaths.

Some argue that antismoking ads, such as this one portraying tobacco icon Joe Camel as a bedridden cancer patient, greatly exaggerate the risks of smoking.

The extent to which secondhand smoke poses a health risk to nonsmokers is hotly debated.

Marimont and Levy also found no adjustments were made to the costs of smoking resulting from the benefits of smoking—reduced Alzheimer's and Parkinson's disease, less obesity, depression and breast cancer. . . .

Fraudulent Science

If both the chemical constituents of tobacco smoke and the numbers of smoking-related deaths are overstated—and clearly they are—how can we trust the claim that tobacco smoke is harmful to non-smokers?

The 1993 bellwether study by the Environmental Protection Agency that selectively combined the results of a number of previous studies and found a small increase in lung cancer risk in those exposed to environmental tobacco smoke has been roundly criticized as severely flawed by fellow researchers and ultimately found invalid in a court of law.

In 1998, the World Health Organization reported a small, but not statistically significant, increase in the risk of lung cancer in non-smoking women married to smokers.

Despite these invalidating deficiencies, the Environmental Protection Agency and World Health Organization both concluded tobacco smoke causes lung cancer in non-smokers.

One wonders whether the same conclusions would have been announced if scientific fraud were a criminal offence.

Overstating the Risks of Smoking Is Dangerous

When confronted with the scientific uncertainty, the inconsistency of results and the incredible misrepresentation of present-day knowledge, those seeking to abolish tobacco invoke a radical interpretation of the Precautionary Principle: "Where potential adverse effects are not fully understood, the activity should not proceed."

This unreasonable exploitation of the ever-present risks of living infiltrates our schools to indoctrinate trusting and eager minds with the irrational fears of today. Instead of opening minds to the wondrous complexities of living, it opens the door to peer ridicule and intolerance while cultivating the trendy cynics of tomorrow.

If we continue down this dangerous path of control and prohibition based on an unreliable or remote chance of harm, how many personal freedoms will remain seven generations from now?

EVALUATING THE AUTHOR'S ARGUMENTS:

In the viewpoint you just read, author Eric Boyd claims that overstating the risks of smoking could set America on a "dangerous path of control and prohibition" that would result in a loss of freedom. What is your assessment of this claim? Do you think it is realistic or unrealistic? Explain your answer using evidence from the viewpoints you have read.

Secondhand Smoke Is Harmful to Health

Bob Doyle and Angela Hudson

"Secondhand smoke . . . contains more than 4,000 chemicals. More than 100 of those are poisonous and 43 are known carcinogens."

In the following viewpoint, Bob Doyle and Angela Hudson argue that the tobacco industry has gone to great lengths to obscure what they contend is an undeniable truth: that secondhand cigarette smoke is hazardous to human health. From pushing ventilation systems to advertising in political magazines, the authors charge the tobacco industry with attempting to deceive the American public on the dangers of secondhand smoke so their profits will not be lessened. The authors argue that secondhand smoke is a known killer, and cite statistics compiled by the Environmental Protection Agency that suggest thousands of people die from secondhand smoke per year. Furthermore, cigarette smoke contains thousands of chemicals, some of which are known to cause cancer. The authors conclude that secondhand smoke is hazardous to human health, and Americans should not allow themselves to be deceived on this issue by the tobacco companies.

Bob Doyle is the director of Tobacco Control Programs for the American Lung Association of Colorado. Angela Hudson is the community health coordinator for the State Tobacco Education and Prevention Partnership of the El Paso Department of Public Health.

AS YOU READ, CONSIDER THE FOLLOWING QUESTIONS:
1. According to the authors, why does a company like Philip Morris fear smoke-free environments?
2. What was the content of the program tobacco company Philip Morris called "Options"?
3. According to the authors, how many Americans die from secondhand smoke per year?

After decades of manufacturing myths that smoking wasn't a health danger, the tobacco giants are at it again, using the same campaign tactics to create a smokescreen around the hazards of second-hand smoke. In Colorado Springs and throughout Colorado, [tobacco giant] Philip Morris is targeting the business community and elected officials by advocating ventilation technologies to

Several states have banned smoking in public places in order to reduce people's exposure to second-hand smoke.

circumvent the real issue of the toxins in tobacco smoke. The issue is heating up as more communities implement smoke-free policies for public places.

The tobacco companies are again disseminating misleading information that obscures the clear-cut scientific consensus regarding the dangers of second-hand smoke. Philip Morris, the world's largest manufacturer of cigarettes, has created a program called "Options" to encourage owners of bars, restaurants, and bowling alleys to upgrade ventilation systems as a solution to the effects of second-hand smoke.

Second-Hand Smoke Kills

In Colorado, Philip Morris is funding the Colorado Indoor Air Coalition to promote the program and placing ads in *The Colorado Statesman,* a publication for Colorado elected officials. The coalition recently sent out fliers to members of the Colorado Restaurant Association, promoting ventilation to "accommodate smokers and non-smokers." The mailing makes no mention of the health impacts that patrons and employees suffer from second-hand smoke. But the science is unequivocal, according to James Repace, national second-hand smoke expert and former senior science policy analyst for the Environmental Protection Agency (EPA). "There is no safe level of exposure to second-hand smoke and no ventilation system has been able to eliminate the health risks due to second-hand smoke," he states. Second-hand smoke poses serious health risks: it is a major source of indoor air pollution, and contains more than 4,000 chemicals. More than 100 of those are poisonous and 43 are known carcinogens—cancer-causing substances.

Every year second-hand smoke causes 3,000 deaths by lung cancer and more than 37,000 deaths by coronary disease, making it the third leading cause of preventable death in the United States, according to the EPA. Internal tobacco industry files, released in the 1998 Master

FAST FACT

Research conducted by the University of California shows that less than thirty minutes of exposure to secondhand smoke reduces the function of a person's coronary arteries. After thirty minutes of exposure to secondhand smoke, the endothelium, the lining of the arteries, functions at the same level as that of a regular smoker.

IF YOU SMOKE AROUND YOUR
CHILDREN, THEY CAN INHALE
THE EQUIVALENT OF 102 PACKS
OF CIGARETTES BY AGE 5.

SECONDHAND SMOKE. STILL WANT TO BREATHE IT?

In 2001 three-dimensional antismoking displays, such as this one illustrating the effects of second-hand smoke on children, began appearing throughout Minneapolis.

Settlement Agreement between the states and tobacco companies, show that the industry knew for years about the health risks of second-hand smoke. Philip Morris' response to the medical evidence was to develop a campaign of deception, clearly outlined in a 1995 strategy paper, "Indoor Air Quality: An Alternative Strategy," promoting ventilation as a way to deflect the mounting evidence against second-hand smoke.

Tobacco Companies Want to Deceive the Public

Why has the tobacco industry worked to obscure the scientific evidence? The first goal, stated in a once-confidential 1989 Philip Morris document, is to "defeat mandatory and voluntary smoking restrictions" and "slow the decline of social acceptability of smoking." Philip Morris more recently has turned to public relations and political initiatives around the U.S. to achieve its goals, lobbying city councils and state legislatures to draft laws encouraging the use of ventilation to counter the smoke-free movement.

The Philip Morris company has aggressively lobbied city and state officials to draft ventilation laws rather than ban smoking in public places.

The second reason tobacco companies oppose smoke-free environments is revealed in a 1992 internal memo from Philip Morris, stating that smoke-free workplace policies were associated with a decline in daily cigarette consumption and a higher quit rate for smokers. Another 1993 confidential Philip Morris document reveals the firm's concern that clean indoor air legislation in the United States could reduce cigarette sales in that year by $40 million.

The evidence is clear. The only industry that suffers when homes, businesses, and communities go smoke-free is the tobacco industry itself, which puts profits before people. This is the industry that has put millions of dollars into deceptive public relations efforts to divert the public and the hospitality industry from the real issue of second-hand smoke: the health of the American public. Coloradans should not be deceived by the tobacco industry's latest smokescreen.

EVALUATING THE AUTHORS' ARGUMENTS:

In the viewpoint you just read, the authors argue that secondhand smoke is harmful based on studies that show it has toxic effects on the body. In the following viewpoint, the author argues that secondhand smoke is not a health hazard based on different studies that have concluded this. How might you account for the discrepancy between these two opposing viewpoints? Which conclusion do you agree with more, and why? Explain your answer.

The Effects of Secondhand Smoke Have Been Exaggerated

Gene Healy

"Secondhand smoke is, at worst, a minuscule health risk that is easily avoided."

In the following viewpoint, author Gene Healy argues that the health effects of secondhand smoke have been greatly exaggerated by an overly alarmed and interfering nonsmoking public that hopes to completely eradicate smoking from American life. He says no clear evidence links secondhand smoke exposure to damaged health, and suggests that studies that have shown the opposite have been flawed or declared invalid by the courts. The author also argues that secondhand smoke is an easily avoidable nuisance; people can simply not be around smokers, and those who work as bartenders or waitresses can choose to take employment in the growing number of establishments that have volunteered to become smoke free. The author concludes by saying that people have exaggerated the health risks posed by secondhand smoke in order to demonize smoking.

Gene Healy, "Healthy Living Through Coercion," *The Washington Times,* December 11, 2003, p. A21.

Gene Healy is senior editor at the Cato Institute, a nonprofit public policy research foundation that favors limited government.

AS YOU READ, CONSIDER THE FOLLOWING QUESTIONS:
1. What do you think the author means when he refers to "secondhand lead poisoning"?
2. What is the Smokefree Workplaces Act of 2003?
3. What did the *British Medical Journal* conclude about secondhand smoke on the basis of data collected on Californians?

On Dec. 3 [2003] in a contentious public hearing, the [Washington] D.C. City Council heard testimony for and against the Smokefree Workplaces Act of 2003, a bill that would ban smoking in all District bars and restaurants. With the District reclaiming its title as murder capital of the United States, one might think the city council would have more pressing issues to deal with, such as secondhand lead poisoning in the form of stray bullets.

But supporters of the ban argue secondhand smoke is a life or death public health issue. In fact, Smokefree D.C., the activist group backing the ban, claims environmental tobacco smoke kills up to 65,000 Americans a year—more than 3 times the national murder rate. But they're fudging the facts. Their real goal is to socially engineer smoking out of existence.

FAST FACT

A 1998 study conducted by the World Health Organization found no statistically significant increased lung cancer risk for nonsmokers who were exposed to cigarette smoke in their homes, workplaces, vehicles, or restaurants.

There Is No Evidence That Secondhand Smoke Harms

The epidemiological evidence doesn't come close to justifying the outlandish claim secondhand smoke kills more people than handguns. Since "the dose makes the poison," it's far from clear that passive inhalation of secondhand smoke poses any significantly increased health risk at all. The Environmental

Protection Agency's attempt to show it does was thrown out of court as junk science by a federal district court judge in 1998. A study released in May [2002] in the *British Medical Journal* used American Cancer Society data tracking 35,561 Californians over 39 years, and concluded, "The results do not support a causal relation between environmental tobacco smoke [ETS] and tobacco-related mortality."

Secondhand smoke is, at worst, a minuscule health risk that is easily avoided. There are plenty of employment opportunities for service industry workers who prefer not to be exposed to ETS. Smokefree D.C.'s Web page features a list of 261 restaurants, bars and coffee shops in the D.C. area that have voluntarily decided to go smoke-free. If exposure to secondhand smoke is an intolerable health risk that workers cannot be allowed to assume, then why in the world do we allow people to take jobs delivering pizzas or working as bike messengers, where they might be killed on any given day?

The push for a D.C. smoking ban isn't really about protecting workers. Antismoking activists make unsupportable claims about the health risks of ETS to advance their real goal: reducing the number

Source: Myers. © by Tribune Media Services. Reproduced by permission.

of cigarette smokers by reducing the number of places in which one can legally smoke.

Nonsmokers Are Bent on Eliminating Smoking

At one time, this was a private strategy of the antismoking movement. At a 1986 antismoking conference, Stanton Glantz, director of the Center for Tobacco Control Research and Education, explained: "Although the nonsmokers' rights movement concentrates on protecting the nonsmoker rather than on urging the smoker to quit for his or her own benefit, clean indoor air legislation reduces smoking

In 2003 former surgeon general David Satcher, seen here delivering the results of a 1998 smoking study, endorsed a push to ban smoking in restaurants and bars in Washington, D.C.

Smokers' rights advocates view the growing number of smoke-free public spaces, like this park, as part of a campaign to make smoking socially unacceptable.

because it undercuts the social support network for smoking by implicitly defining smoking as an antisocial act."

But antismoking activists are becoming increasingly brazen about their desire to coerce smokers into quitting. On Nov. 18 [2003], the Robert Wood Johnson Foundation, the New Jersey–based public health group that has donated a quarter-million dollars to the drive for a D.C. smoking ban, ran an eight-page advertising supplement in the *New York Times*. The cover features a scene from the inside of a smoke-free bar, with glamorous twentysomethings chatting and drinking martinis. Through the bar's window, you can see a forlorn group of smokers huddled in the rain and shivering. The caption reads: "No longer cool, smokers find themselves out in the cold."

David Satcher, the former surgeon general, echoed this theme in his testimony before the D.C. City Council. He argued the smoking ban would "be effective in creating a new social norm that discourages people from smoking."

Secondhand Smoke Is Unpleasant, but Not Lethal

However desirable that social norm might be, Dr. Satcher and Smokefree D.C. have no right to promote it by restricting the freedom of business owners to set the rules for the premises they own. And they have no right to push adults out into the cold for the sin of indulging in a perfectly legal product.

You may think smoking is a nasty habit and secondhand smoke is unpleasant. But what's truly obnoxious is the drive to make us all healthier people through the coercive arm of the law. That's the impulse behind the D.C. smoking ban, and it has no place in a free, tolerant and diverse city.

EVALUATING THE AUTHOR'S ARGUMENTS:

In the article you just read, author Gene Healy suggests that those living in the Washington, D.C., area have more pressing issues to worry about than any danger from secondhand smoke. In your opinion, how serious is the problem of secondhand smoke? Do you think it should take priority over other social issues that face American communities? Use your knowledge of this matter to fully explain your answer.

Smokeless Tobacco Is Harmful to Health

John DiConsiglio

"Bad breath. Rotting teeth. Cancer. These are just some of the health hazards brought on by chewing tobacco."

John DiConsiglio is the author of six books, including *Young Americans: Tales of Teenage Immigrants* and *Lost Boys of Sudan*. In the following viewpoint, DiConsiglio argues that smokeless or chewing tobacco products are hazardous to human health. Enormously addictive, smokeless tobacco products contain very high concentrations of nicotine, which hook users quickly. He writes that extended use of chewing tobacco causes a variety of cancers, including cancer of the esophagus, pharynx, larynx, and stomach. Furthermore, chewing tobacco wreaks havoc on the mouth, destroying the lips, tongue, teeth, and gums. The author accuses tobacco companies of marketing smokeless tobacco products to teens by making candy-flavored chew products that are specifically designed to appeal to young people. He concludes by saying teens must be taught to reject smokeless tobacco products before they do serious damage to their health.

AS YOU READ, CONSIDER THE FOLLOWING QUESTIONS:
1. According to the article, how many cancer-causing agents are found in chewing tobacco?
2. How many of America's chewing tobacco users are under the age of twenty-one?
3. What are leukoplakia?

Jonathan Grozinger was a dipper. Since he was 11 Jonathan regularly pulled a pinch of chewing tobacco out of a metal tin and tucked it between his cheek and gum. By his teen years, Jonathan was rarely seen without a wad of the coarse, grainy powder stuffed into his swollen cheek. "My mouth just felt empty without some chew sloshing around it," says Jonathan, now 17.

"My Gums Were Raw, Swollen, and Bleeding"

His girlfriend found the habit disgusting. She hated the way Jonathan constantly spit the tobacco's black juices. And she made him brush his teeth before he came near her.

"It's hard to get a kiss from a girl when you've got tobacco grains in your teeth," Jonathan says. His family tried to get him to stop. But in his small Arkansas town, everyone seemed to be chewing—from the friends he went four-wheeling with to the cowboys in the tobacco-sponsored rodeos.

Besides, once Jonathan became hooked on the doses of nicotine in each pinch of chew, quitting wasn't easy. Nicotine, which is also in cigarettes, is a potent chemical that makes the person chewing the tobacco addicted to the substance. Once inside your body, nicotine is absorbed into your bloodstream and travels to your brain. At this point, it creates feelings of pleasure in your body.

But that feeling doesn't last long, and once it's gone, your body wants it back. So you put more chewing tobacco in your mouth. "I didn't think chewing was that bad at first," Jonathan says. "I never thought I'd get addicted to it. But the more I did it, the more I couldn't go without it."

One person Jonathan finally listened to was his dentist. Last spring, Jonathan made an appointment to have his teeth cleaned. The dentist gasped when he looked inside Jonathan's mouth.

"My gums were raw, swollen, and bleeding," Jonathan says. "My dentist said it was the worst mouth he'd ever seen in a person my age. He told me, 'Jonathan, if you keep chewing that stuff, you may get cancer. And you'll definitely lose all your teeth.'"

Addictive and Accessible

Bad breath. Rotting teeth. Cancer. These are just some of the health hazards brought on by chewing tobacco, which is also called spit, snuff, or dip. Still, nearly one in five male high school students chews tobacco. In many parts of the United States, the worn rings that spit-tobacco tins form in the pockets of jeans have become a status symbol for teens.

Unlike smoking, many teens chew through the school day without anyone knowing. "I would do it in class and no one ever bothered me," says Jonathan, who finally quit and has been off chew for three

Studies show that nearly one in five male high school students, such as this baseball player, chews tobacco.

months. "You couldn't spit the juices on the floor. So I'd have to swallow them."

Besides being addictive, chewing tobacco is also accessible to teens. "It's easier to get than alcohol and cigarettes," says Matt Van Wyck, a former chewer who now runs the QuitSmokeless.org Web site. "I get so many e-mails from teens who say they started chewing and can't quit."

While there are several kinds of chewing tobacco, the most popular is snuff. Snuff is a finely ground or shredded form of tobacco that

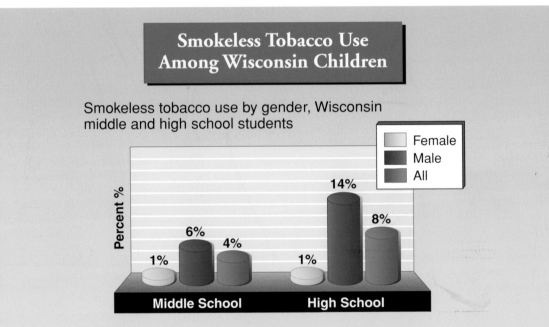

Smokeless Tobacco Use Among Wisconsin Children

Smokeless tobacco use by gender, Wisconsin middle and high school students

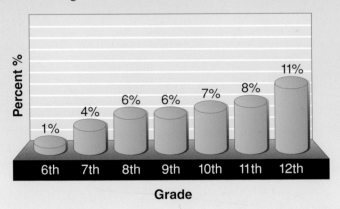

Smokeless tobacco use by grade, Wisconsin middle and high school students

Source: Wisconsin Youth Tobacco Survey, Department of Health and Family Services/Division of Public Health/Bureau of Chronic Disease Prevention, 2000.

chewers hold between their lip or cheek and gums. Thick tobacco juice forms in the mouth, which chewers must constantly spit out.

Smokeless Tobacco Users Are Prone to Cancer

Since the so-called smokeless tobacco is not inhaled, many teens think it is safe. But in some ways, chewing tobacco is even more dangerous than cigarettes. Snuff contains at least 28 cancer-causing agents. And the amount of nicotine in one pinch of dip can be four times as high as the nicotine in a single cigarette. As the moist chew is held in the mouth, nicotine seeps through your gums and into your bloodstream.

"There's really nasty stuff in chew," says Ross Rayson of the Dental Health Foundation. "Part of what's in there is a ground-up fiberglass like substance that scratches your gum so the nicotine gets in your blood faster."

That's why chewers often develop burning spots in their mouth, Payson says, and must shift the wad until they find a location that doesn't hurt.

A chewer also develops painful white lesions on his or her tongue, called leukoplakia. The lesions can become cancerous at any time. People who use spit tobacco are 50 times more likely to develop cancer than nonusers. The constant exposure to the tobacco juice causes cancer of the esophagus, pharynx, larynx, and even the stomach. Perhaps worst of all are oral cancers—cancer of the mouth and tongue, for example. Often, the only way to combat these cancers is through surgery that removes large parts of the user's face.

The nicotine in spit tobacco makes it as addictive as cigarettes. People who try to quit chewing tobacco suffer through the same withdrawal symptoms—anxiety, sleeplessness, intense cravings—as heavy smokers. To kick his habit, Jonathan filled his mouth with candy and gum. "I had to always be chewing something," he says. "And even then I wanted to chew tobacco really badly."

Smokeless Tobacco Is Marketed to Teens

Despite the risks, teens are chewing tobacco in frightening numbers. Of the nation's 10 million spit tobacco users, 3 million are under the age of 21. And more than 14 percent of high school boys say they have used spit tobacco in the last month. "It's pretty obvious that teens aren't getting the message that this can kill you," says Danny McGoldrick of the Campaign for Tobacco Free Kids.

Instead, many teens seem to be listening to tobacco companies. Despite lawsuits and legal restrictions on the advertising and sale of chewing tobacco to teens, snuff sales have soared. Annual sales of chewing tobacco top $1.7 billion. And tobacco companies spend $127 million a year on advertising.

A teenager wears a cap advertising a popular brand of smokeless tobacco.

Spit-tobacco companies distribute free tins on college campuses. They sponsor rodeos, concerts, and racing events. And, until recently, they supplied major league baseball teams with hefty supplies of chew. More than 35 percent of baseball players use spit tobacco, although the sport has banned it from the minor leagues and the All-Star game.

Most insidious of all may be the tobacco companies' plan to hook young people on chew. In 1993, the *Wall Street Journal* learned that tobacco companies targeted young chewers with "starter" packs of dip that contained cherry flavoring and lower nicotine levels.

One company document outlined the strategy to hook kids. "Cherry chew is for somebody who likes the taste of candy—if you know what I mean," the document said. The starter-chew tasted better than the full-strength spit tobacco. Once teens got used to the mild chew, they were ready to try chew products that had higher concentrations of nicotine.

That's how Joel McCormick of Glide, Oregon, became addicted to spit tobacco. "I hated the stuff my friends were chewing" says Joel, 16, "But I tried some of the cherry chews and they tasted OK." Before long, Joel was chewing a can a day. That's when his grandfather, a former chewer, took him to meet a friend who had chewed for years. "This guy's gums were all white and cracked. And his whole lower lip was gone," Joel says. "I didn't want that to be me. I went home and threw out all my tins."

EVALUATING THE AUTHORS' ARGUMENTS:

In the viewpoint you just read, author John DiConsiglio describes the various health hazards associated with smokeless tobacco products. In the following viewpoint, author Stephen Chapman acknowledges that smokeless tobacco products can cause oral cancer, but recommends that they be used as a less dangerous alternative to cigarettes. After reading both viewpoints, what is your opinion on smokeless tobacco products? Use evidence from the articles you read to make your point.

Smokeless Tobacco Is Less Harmful than Smoking

Stephen Chapman

"Snuff and other unsmoked forms of tobacco are not nearly as risky as the kind you ignite and inhale."

In the following viewpoint, author Stephen Chapman argues that smokeless tobacco products are less harmful than cigarettes and smokers should be encouraged to use them. Because smokeless tobacco allows a smoker to get a nicotine fix without inhaling toxic chemicals, he contends it is a much safer habit than smoking. In fact, he claims that if all current smokers were to switch to smokeless tobacco products, there would be hundreds of thousands of fewer deaths in the United States. In addition, smokeless tobacco is better than cigarettes because it does not expose nonsmokers to secondhand smoke. The author concludes by arguing that because people are unlikely to completely abandon nicotine products, they should switch to smokeless tobacco for a healthier and safer experience.

Syndicated columnist Stephen Chapman writes on national and international affairs for the *Chicago Tribune,* from which this viewpoint was taken.

AS YOU READ, CONSIDER THE FOLLOWING QUESTIONS:
1. What point is the author trying to make by comparing smoking to needle-exchange programs?
2. How many lives does the author suggest could be saved if smokers were to switch to smokeless tobacco products?
3. What does the author mean when he describes smokeless tobacco as "second best"?

It's been 40 years since the surgeon general issued the first report warning that cigarettes cause cancer. Since then, the public has grown acutely aware that smoking is lethal. But though the public education campaign has been a great success in providing information, it's been a failure in one conspicuous way: 46 million American adults still smoke.

How come? Because it's so hard to quit. Nicotine is so powerfully addictive that lots of people find it impossible to give up—even with lung cancer, emphysema and heart disease staring them in the face. Despite an array of products and strategies designed to help people conquer the habit, cigarettes remain a major killer in this country.

Because smokeless tobacco is not inhaled, some claim it is less of a health risk than smoked tobacco.

Smokeless Tobacco Can Reduce Smoking Deaths

If we want to know how to reduce the health toll from tobacco use, we might want to look at Sweden, where smoking among men has dropped sharply in recent years. How come? Brad Rodu, a professor of pathology at the University of Alabama at Birmingham, says one big reason is that a lot of Swedish smokers have switched to smokeless tobacco.

That may sound like a pointless exercise, substituting one deadly addiction for another. In fact, snuff and other unsmoked forms of tobacco are not nearly as risky as the kind you ignite and inhale.

A 2002 report by Britain's Royal College of Physicians noted that "the consumption of non-combustible tobacco is of the order of 10 to 1,000 times less hazardous than smoking." Smokeless tobacco is known to cause oral cancer. But Rodu estimates that if everyone now smoking made the change, the annual number of tobacco-related deaths in the United States would plunge from 440,000 to 6,000.

A man buys a tin of chewing tobacco from a vending machine in Sweden. Such machines are becoming popular in places where smoking has been banned.

Help Smokers Help Themselves

U.S. Surgeon General Richard Carmona, who says he would like to ban all tobacco products, insists that "there is no scientific evidence that smokeless tobacco products are both safe and effective aids to quitting smoking." Anti-smoking groups portray smokeless tobacco as an intolerable danger. But a growing pile of evidence suggests snuff could be a valuable tool to help smokers help themselves.

It's true that they'd do well to swear off the weed in any form. But when virtue fails, as it often does, we have to look for ways to make vice less dangerous. That's the rationale for giving teens access to condoms and other types of birth control, even if we strongly prefer that they abstain from sex. It's also the idea behind needle-exchange programs, which recognize that one thing worse than injecting heroin is injecting it with an AIDS-infected syringe.

> **FAST FACT**
>
> According to Terrence Scanlon, former chairman of the U.S. Consumer Product Safety Commission, smoking is seventy times more lethal than chewing tobacco.

Smokeless tobacco offers hope to hard-core smokers because it lets them fill their nicotine needs without sucking toxic fumes into their lungs. Addicts would be better off getting their daily dose without lighting up.

The rest of us would gain as well, since this indulgence lacks a notable byproduct of cigarettes: secondhand smoke. (With some forms, the user doesn't even have to spit.) And nobody ever burned down his house by falling asleep while dipping snuff.

You may wonder why any smoker wouldn't use nicotine gum or patches instead. Answer: because they're more expensive and less potent, relieving smokers of their cash but not their cravings. While nicotine maintenance works for some people, it doesn't work for others, and they shouldn't be deprived of additional options.

Smokeless Tobacco Is Second Best

Critics dismiss Rodu as a hired gun for the smokeless tobacco industry, which in recent years has donated money to support his research

Although chewing tobacco is known to cause oral cancer, it does not cause lung cancer in the same way that cigarettes do.

and would like to market its product as a safer alternative to smoking. But he says his studies between 1993 and 1999 were done without any industry financing. The funds the industry has given since then have been unrestricted grants to the University of Alabama at Birmingham, and it has no control over the research.

Attacking his funding seems to be easier than refuting his evidence. If the tobacco industry donates money to scientists who say the sky is blue, that doesn't make it green. Instead of rejecting the scientific data that has been produced on the subject, the surgeon general should be demanding government funding for additional research.

Based on the evidence so far, though, smokeless tobacco is far less dangerous than cigarettes, and the industry should be free to publicize that fact. The ideal solution, of course, is for everyone who smokes to quit tobacco once and for all. But when people can't or won't do what's best for them, we shouldn't discourage them from doing what's second best.

EVALUATING THE AUTHOR'S ARGUMENTS:

In the viewpoint you just read, the author suggests that because many smokers are unlikely to be able to quit smoking, it is better for them to switch to smokeless tobacco than to not change their habit at all. This rationale has been applied to other social issues as a way to effect change in a difficult situation. For example, it is frequently argued that since teenagers are likely to have sex, it is better to equip them with knowledge of how to prevent disease and pregnancy than to teach them only abstinence. Do you think that this is a useful method for effecting change? Or, do you believe solutions based on such compromises do not adequately address the problem at hand? Explain your position.

CHAPTER 2

What Causes People to Smoke?

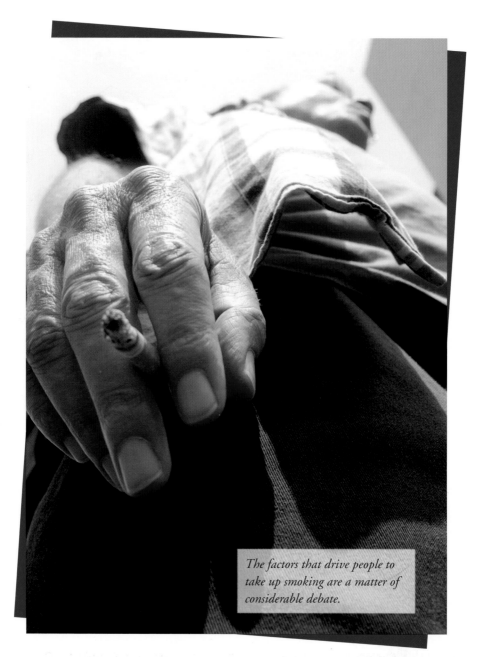

The factors that drive people to take up smoking are a matter of considerable debate.

The Tobacco Industry Encourages Young People to Smoke

Campaign for Tobacco-Free Kids

In the following viewpoint, the Campaign for Tobacco-Free Kids argues that despite restrictions placed on the tobacco industry, cigarette manufacturers continue to bombard kids with advertising to encourage them to smoke. The organization cites data that show teenagers are three times more likely to recall cigarette advertising than adults, implying that they are exposed to much more of it. In addition, the organization suggests that it remains easy for children to obtain cigarettes, despite the tobacco companies' claims that they have clamped down on sales to minors. The Campaign for Tobacco-Free Kids concludes that the tobacco industry has violated the stipulations of the 1998 Master Settlement Agreement, which prohibited them from marketing their product to young people.

"Kids are at the center of the bulls-eye for Marlboro."

Campaign for Tobacco-Free Kids, "New Poll Shows Kids Still Bombarded with Tobacco Advertising," www.tobaccofreekids.org, April 3, 2002.

The Campaign for Tobacco-Free Kids is a nonprofit organization whose goal is to protect children from tobacco addiction and exposure to secondhand smoke.

AS YOU READ, CONSIDER THE FOLLOWING QUESTIONS:
1. According to the article, what is significant about teens believing that 62 percent of high school students smoke, when in fact just 28 percent do?
2. What methods does William V. Corr suggest in order to stop tobacco marketing to children?
3. According to the article, of the two thousand kids a day who become regular smokers, how many die as a result?

More than three years after the major tobacco companies agreed to stop marketing to kids as part of the 1998 state tobacco settlement, a new poll shows that kids are twice as likely as adults to be exposed to tobacco advertising. The poll, conducted for the Campaign for Tobacco-Free Kids in March [2002], also finds that three-quarters of kids feel targeted by tobacco companies, kids overestimate the proportion of teens and adults who smoke, and they still find it relatively easy to buy tobacco products.

The poll was released as thousands of kids across America rally against tobacco on [April 3, 2002], the seventh annual Kick Butts Day.

FAST FACT

According to a study done by the University of Chicago, in the two years following the 1998 Master Settlement Agreement, tobacco companies increased their ads in magazines such as *Glamour* by 14 percent; 1.9 million *Glamour* readers are between the ages of twelve and seventeen.

"Hypocrisy and Duplicity"

The poll found that nearly two-thirds (64 percent) of youth aged 12 to 17 say they have seen advertising for cigarettes or spit tobacco products in the previous two weeks, compared to only 27 percent of adults who claim to have seen such ads.

Philip Morris' Marlboro is by far the brand whose advertising most often leaves a mark on kids. Among those who recall tobacco advertising, 61 percent of kids, compared to 49 percent of adults, recall advertising for Marlboro. Among all survey respondents (regardless of whether they recall any ads), 39 percent of the youth surveyed and just 13 percent of adults recall Marlboro advertising from the last two weeks. Thus, youth are three times as likely as adults to recall Marlboro advertising. It is no wonder then that Marlboro, the most heavily advertised brand, is by far the brand of choice among youth smokers. According to the National Household Survey on Drug Abuse, more youth smokers (55 percent) smoke Marlboro than all other brands combined.

"This poll exposes the tobacco companies' hypocrisy and duplicity when they say they have changed their marketing and do not want kids to smoke," said Matthew L. Myers, President of the Campaign for Tobacco-Free Kids. "Philip Morris, the tobacco company that claims to be doing the most to prevent youth smoking, is doing the worst job of all. If Philip Morris isn't aiming at children, they better fire their ad agency because this survey shows that kids are at the center of the bulls-eye for Marlboro."

Source: Auth. © 1996 by *The Philadelphia Inquirer.* Reproduced by permission of Universal Press Syndicate.

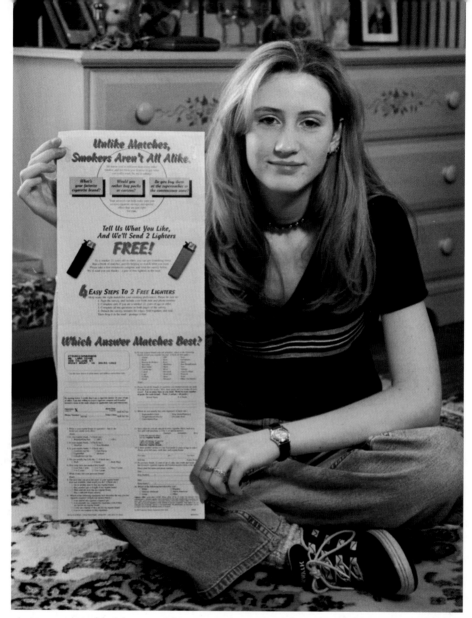

A sixteen-year-old girl poses with a survey she received from the Philip Morris company, which offers her two free lighters for completing the survey.

"The tobacco industry's marketing to our children will not be stopped until Congress grants the U.S. Food and Drug Administration authority over tobacco products, including the authority to prohibit marketing that appeals to kids. State leaders also must do more to protect kids by increasing cigarette taxes and funding effective, comprehensive tobacco prevention programs. These are proven solutions that can protect kids from tobacco use and the addiction, disease and death that results," said William V. Corr, Executive Vice President of the Campaign for Tobacco-Free Kids.

Tobacco Ads Create Sense of Acceptance

Given the high level of exposure to tobacco marketing found by the poll, it is not surprising that 71 percent of the youth surveyed feel that tobacco companies want teens to smoke and that 76 percent believe tobacco companies target teens with their advertising.

This ubiquity of tobacco marketing—over $8.2 billion annually, according to the most recent Federal Trade Commission [FTC] report—also creates an environment in which teens think smoking is much more common, and thus acceptable, than it actually is. According to the new survey, youth believe that about 62 percent of high school students are current smokers when, in fact, about 28 percent are. Similarly, the youth surveyed believe that about 64 percent

A New York teen walks past the window of a neighborhood liquor store plastered with colorful tobacco ads.

of adults smoke, when national surveys show an adult smoking rate of 23 percent.

Finally, youth still think it is relatively easy for minors to buy cigarettes and other tobacco products. Seventy percent of the youth surveyed said it is easy for people under age 18 to buy tobacco products. Sixty-three percent said it is easy for people under age 18 to buy tobacco products on the Internet.

The False Claims of Big Tobacco

As part of the November 1998 state tobacco settlement, the tobacco companies promised not to "take any action, directly or indirectly, to target youth." The tobacco companies have also spent hundreds of millions of dollars on public relations campaigns claiming they are reformed. However, several studies since the settlement, including the FTC report, found that the tobacco companies increased their marketing expenditures to record levels after the settlement and that they shifted expenditures to forms of advertising, such as magazines and convenience stores, that are most effective at reaching kids.

Tobacco use is the leading preventable cause of death in the United States, killing more than 400,000 Americans every year. Ninety percent of all smokers start at or before age 18. Every day, 5,000 kids try their first cigarette. Another 2,000 kids become regular, daily smokers, one-third of whom will die prematurely as a result.

EVALUATING THE AUTHORS' ARGUMENTS:

The viewpoint you just read is written by an antismoking organization whose goal is to prevent young people from becoming addicted to cigarettes. Robert A. Levy, the author of the following viewpoint, is a member of a think tank that adheres to libertarianism, a political philosophy that advocates limited government regulation of business. How should the background of these authors influence your reaction to their position? Explain your answer.

Tobacco Industry Advertising Is Not Responsible for Teen Smoking

Robert A. Levy

"Cigarette ads are not the problem."

In the following viewpoint, Robert A. Levy responds to accusations by tobacco industry critics, including California state attorney general Bill Lockyer. Lockyer and others have charged tobacco companies with violating past legal promises and targeting youth in their marketing campaigns. Levy argues that tobacco companies are not specifically targeting young people when they place advertisements in magazines like *TV Guide* and *People*. He adds that extensive investigations by the Justice Department have failed to uncover evidence of marketing to minors. Levy further contends that tobacco advertising has little influence on whether teens begin to smoke. Other causes such as peer pressure and parental role models have a greater effect on teen smoking. Levy is a senior fellow in constitutional studies at the Cato Institute, an organization that opposes many government regulations.

AS YOU READ, CONSIDER THE FOLLOWING QUESTIONS:
1. According to Levy, why should a *New England Journal of Medicine* study on tobacco advertising be viewed with skepticism?
2. Why was Philip Morris more eager than other tobacco companies to curb its magazine advertising, according to the author?
3. What is the purpose of cigarette ads, according to the author?

E xuding self-righteousness, California [attorney general] Bill Lockyer has pounced on tobacco companies for running cigarette ads in magazines like *People, Sports Illustrated* and *TV Guide.* Lockyer's fulmination, triggered by the release of a study in The *New England Journal of Medicine,* came in the wake of his lawsuit against [tobacco company] R.J. Reynolds for having "continuously and systematically targeted youth" by advertising in magazines with substantial teen readership.

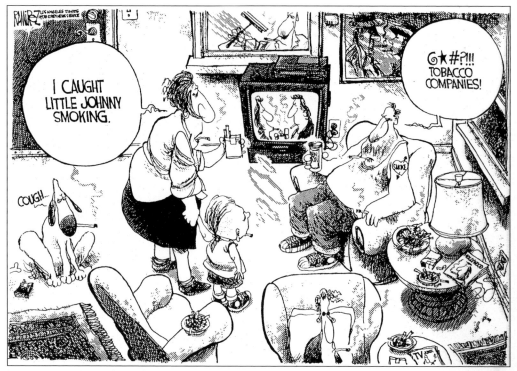

Source: Ramirez. © 1997 by Copley News Service. Reproduced by permission.

Philip Morris executives hold a press conference in 1996. In recent years, the company has funded a number of programs to help keep tobacco out of the hands of minors.

The attorney general didn't find it necessary to inform Californians that the study was partly funded by a public official now suing a tobacco company. Nor did Lockyer mention that the study's co-author is a long-time activist and former board member of California's rabidly anti-tobacco clique, Americans for Nonsmokers' Rights. . . .

Lockyer complains that the [1998] multistate settlement agreement [between states and the tobacco industry] proscribes cigarette ads in magazines read by lots of kids. In fact, the settlement only commits the industry not to target underage smokers.

Tobacco Companies Curtailed Their Ads

That amorphous provision—in stark contrast to specific bans in the settlement on billboards and bus ads—has been interpreted different-

Instead of curbing a company's right to advertise its product, some argue that strictly checking IDs is the best way to prevent underage smoking.

ly by the several companies. Philip Morris, the market leader, with a vested interest in securing its dominance by restricting competitive advertising, has been almost eager to rein in its magazine ads. The three other tobacco giants also curtailed their ads, but not as aggressively as Philip Morris.

Still, all four companies have surpassed the standard laid down by the Federal Trade Commission, which negotiated a voluntary ban on liquor ads in magazines with more than 30 percent of its readership below the legal drinking age. The FTC, by the way, claims that, "This practice . . . minimizes the number of underage consumers reached by alcohol advertising without unduly interfering with the advertiser's ability to reach a legal-age audience."

FAST FACT

The 1998 Master Settlement Agreement between the tobacco companies and forty-nine states forbids the tobacco companies from marketing their product to young people.

That doesn't impress Lockyer. Neither do the results of a five-year Justice Department investigation that was unable to produce a single indictment of a tobacco executive for marketing to minors, despite painstaking efforts by prosecutors and FBI agents, testimony by whistle-blowers, and disgorgement of millions of new documents.

None of that matters. Rather than more vigorous enforcement of California laws that foreclose the sale of cigarettes to minors, Lockyer has decided that kids will become more responsible if they don't see magazine ads—even if they do see their state's chief law enforcement officer flout the First Amendment in pursuit of his anti-tobacco crusade.

Our constitution protects Klan speech, flag burning and gangsta rap (targeted directly at teen-agers). But if R.J. Reynolds advertises Camel cigarettes in *Sports Illustrated,* which is read overwhelmingly by adults, the boot of Lockyer's state government will come down hard on the company's neck. . . .

Cigarette ads are not the problem. Like automobile ads, they are designed to encourage brand shifting. Indeed, six European countries that have prohibited tobacco ads found that teen consumption increased. Kids smoke because of peer pressure, because their parents smoke and because they are rebelling against authority. Those are the problems that have to be addressed, without violating commercial speech rights and without preventing adults from looking at magazine advertisements.

EVALUATING THE AUTHORS' ARGUMENTS:

In the viewpoint you just read, Robert A. Levy claims that cigarette companies are being responsible in curtailing their advertising to young people and that advertising should not be held responsible for teen smoking. In the previous viewpoint, the Campaign for Tobacco-Free Kids argues that tobacco companies such as Philip Morris continue to target young smokers. After reading both viewpoints, which arguments do you find more persuasive, and why? Explain your answer using evidence from the articles.

Movies Encourage Young People to Smoke

Madeline Dalton

"Eliminating or reducing adolescents' exposure to smoking in movies could significantly reduce the number of adolescents who initiate smoking."

In the following viewpoint, Madeline Dalton argues that movies play a substantial role in encouraging young people to start smoking. She contends that movies greatly influence teenagers; they tend to imitate the habits and tastes of characters they see on the screen. She claims that when teenagers see their favorite actor smoking cigarettes on screen, they are more likely to pick up the habit. She also cites data that show a correlation between the amount of smoking-oriented movies a teenager watches and that teenager's likelihood to start smoking. She concludes that the film industry should reduce the amount of smoking-related content in movies.

Madeline Dalton is an associate professor of pediatrics at Dartmouth Medical School. She was part of a panel of experts who testified before the Senate on the impact of smoking in the media.

Madeline Dalton, testimony before the U.S. Senate Committee on Commerce, Science, and Transportation, Washington, DC, May 11, 2004.

AS YOU READ, CONSIDER THE FOLLOWING QUESTIONS:
1. According to the article, what percentage of PG- and PG-13-rated movies feature smoking?
2. Between what ages does the author say people are most likely to start smoking?
3. According to the author, what are three qualities adolescents associate with smoking?

Good afternoon. My name is Madeline Dalton. I'm an Associate Professor in the Department of Pediatrics and the Norris Cotton Cancer Center at Dartmouth Medical School. For the past 9 years, I've worked with a multi-disciplinary team of investigators studying the influence of behavioral and social risk factors for adolescent smoking. I'm honored to be here today and appreciate the opportunity to share with you the results of our most recent study, which looked at the influence of movies on adolescent smoking behavior.

Adolescents engage in a number of high risk health behaviors, but smoking is of particular concern because it is the leading cause of preventable death in our country. Smoking kills over 400,000 people in the US each year, which is more than the number of deaths caused by alcohol, illicit drugs, motor vehicles, sexual activity and firearms combined. The period of greatest risk for smoking initiation is during childhood, particularly between 10 and 15 years of age. If we can prevent children from smoking until they reach their 18th birthday, then their chance of becoming an addicted smoker is very low. This is the primary reason why we study, and try to prevent, risk factors for smoking initiation during adolescence.

FAST FACT

A 2002 study by Dartmouth University found that young people are sixteen times more likely to use tobacco if their favorite actor does.

Smoking Is Prominent in Teen Movies

Movies are potentially a very important social influence on adolescent smoking. Movies not only depict modern societal norms and styles, they help to define them. In popular contemporary movies, smoking is commonly associated with characteristics many adolescents find appealing, such as toughness, sexiness, and rebelliousness. Cigarette brand appearances and smoking portrayals in movies endorse smoking behavior by associating it with larger-than-life actors, many of whom are social icons for adolescents. Adolescents are vulnerable to these portrayals, as they look to movie stars to help form their own identity and self-image.

In our study, we analyzed the smoking content of 600 top box-office hits released over the past decade. Eighty-five percent of these movies portrayed smoking. Movies were more likely to have smoking as the rating increased. For example, smoking was portrayed in approximately half of G-rated movies compared to 90% of R-rated movies. More than three quarters of PG and PG-13 movies, which are generally considered appropriate for adolescent audiences, featured smoking.

Prior research has shown that adolescents are more likely to smoke if their favorite movie stars smoke on-screen. Experimental studies of

During a 2004 press conference, a Los Angeles County public health official discusses the results of a five-year study on smoking in the movies.

adolescents suggest that viewing smoking in movies is associated with more positive attitudes toward smoking. Our cross-sectional survey of almost 5000 adolescents showed that the more smoking adolescents viewed in movies, the more likely they were to have tried smoking themselves. To validate these findings, we initiated a prospective follow-up study in 2000. The goal of the prospective study was to determine if

This movie poster for a 1960 Italian film portrays the star with a cigarette in his mouth. On-screen smoking is typically associated with sexiness and rebelliousness.

In this scene from the 2002 blockbuster, Men in Black II, *the gun-toting alien on the left enhances his tough-guy image with a cigarette.*

viewing smoking in movies predicted smoking initiation among adolescent never-smokers.

Study Shows Smoking in Movies Influences Teens

The prospective study surveyed adolescents, 10–14 years of age, at 14 middle schools in Northern New England. We asked the students about their movie viewing, smoking behavior, and a number of other factors related to smoking, including peer and family smoking, school performance, child personality characteristics, parent education, parental monitoring, and parental disapproval of smoking. Through this survey, we identified 3547 adolescents who had never tried smoking. We re-contacted 73% (2603) of these adolescents by telephone one to two years after the initial survey to determine if they had initiated smoking. Overall, ten percent (259) of the students had initiated smoking.

Adolescents who saw the most amount of smoking in movies were much more likely to initiate smoking themselves. Seventeen percent (107) of those who had the highest exposure to smoking in movies had initiated smoking, compared to only 3% (22) of those who had the lowest exposure. We recognize that other factors, such as peer and family smoking, child personality characteristics, and parenting characteristics, also influence an adolescent's decision to smoke. We included these in our analysis as possible alternative explanations for smoking initiation. Even after taking all of these factors into account, we found that adolescents who viewed the most smoking in movies were still 2.7 times more likely to try smoking compared to those who viewed the least amount of smoking in movies. The influence of movies on adolescent smoking initiation was greatest among children whose parents did not smoke, showing a four-fold increase in risk of smoking initiation when children with high exposure to movie smoking were compared to those with low exposure. Overall, even after controlling for all of the other factors, we found that half (52.2%) the adolescents who initiated smoking in this study did so because of viewing smoking in movies.

The results of this study confirm prior research by providing strong evidence that viewing smoking in movies promotes smoking initiation among adolescents. Children of non-smoking parents appear to be particularly susceptible to the influence of movie smoking, indicating that modeling non-smoking behavior in the home is not enough to prevent children from initiating smoking. Our findings indicate that eliminating or reducing adolescents' exposure to smoking in movies could significantly reduce the number of adolescents who initiate smoking.

EVALUATING THE AUTHOR'S ARGUMENTS:

In the viewpoint you just read, author Madeline Dalton suggests that smoking in the movies should be curbed in order to reduce the number of teenage smokers. However, it is often argued that it is impossible to portray historically accurate movies, such as those set during World War II or in the Old West, without showing smoking. In your opinion, should the presence of smoking in movies be regulated? Is it more important to capture the details of a particular era or to positively impact viewers? Explain your answer.

Genetics Can Explain Why People Smoke

Tina Hesman

"A combination of genetic factors . . . may determine whether a smoker becomes the one person in three who gets addicted to tobacco."

In the following viewpoint, reporter Tina Hesman describes emerging scientific research that suggests genetics play a role in a person's likelihood to become addicted to cigarettes. She discusses one study that shows nicotine addiction is explained in part by how well a person's genes control the release of dopamine, a chemical in the brain that causes pleasure and is released when a person smokes a cigarette. She reports on another study that suggests a genetic variation of an enzyme called CYP2A6 is responsible for how much nicotine a person can tolerate. People with lower amounts of CYP2A6 are more likely to get sick from cigarettes and so are less likely to become smokers. Although much of the human genome is yet to be fully understood, the author reports that it appears likely that genetic factors contribute to nicotine addiction.

Tina Hesman is a science writer for the *St. Louis Post-Dispatch*, the newspaper from which this viewpoint was taken.

AS YOU READ, CONSIDER THE FOLLOWING QUESTIONS:
1. According to the article, why might blacks smoke fewer cigarettes than whites?
2. What percentage of adult smokers succeed in quitting cigarettes for at least a year?
3. According to the article, what is one role genes play in determining who gets addicted to tobacco?

Jennifer, 18, is a smoker. Her whole family smokes. So do her friends. She knows the consequences—lung cancer, heart disease, death.

"That's why I want to quit," she said.

But it's hard. Really hard. . . .

The problem for Jennifer and millions of other smokers is not a lack of willpower, or even a misguided notion that they can beat the odds. In some people smoking rewires the brain, producing a powerful addiction that may never be entirely cured, experts say.

The U.S. surgeon general released a report 40 years ago linking smoking and cancer, and yet a quarter of the adult population still smokes.

"The people who could quit, quit. Now we're left with a group of really committed smokers," said Laura Bierut, a geneticist at Washington University. Bierut is trying to track down the genetic factors that contribute to alcohol and nicotine addiction.

New research by Bierut and others is only beginning to determine why people smoke, who is likely to become addicted, and why some people can stop while others never seem to be able to put the butt out.

Why Can Some Quit, but Not Others?

Variations in liver enzymes that break down nicotine may influence who becomes a smoker and who doesn't, and cause black smokers to puff on fewer cigarettes than their white counterparts.

People with attention deficit disorder are five times more likely to become smokers than those without it. Nicotine may help them concentrate better.

Some families have a genetic predisposition to become nicotine addicts. Other families are full of social smokers who never become dependent on the drug. Studies are under way to determine the difference. . . .

Like Jennifer, most smokers know the harm tobacco can do and say they want to quit smoking. According to the [2004] Missouri County-Level Study Smoking Cessation Report, about half of adult smokers have quit for a day or more in the past year, and almost 62 percent said they intend to stop smoking in the next six months.

An estimated 35 million smokers try to kick the habit each year, but only about 7 percent succeed in remaining smoke-free for more than a year. Most relapse within a few days of quitting and require multiple attempts before they can give up cigarettes, smoking cessation experts say.

Genes Might Determine Nicotine Addiction

The path to addiction is probably the same, whether the vehicle is nicotine, cocaine, alcohol or other drugs, brain researchers say. All

Recent research links smoking with genetic factors, providing one explanation for why so many smokers have trouble kicking their habit.

drugs of addiction seem to affect a region of the brain known as the nucleus accumbens, and all in the same way—by increasing levels of a feel-good chemical called dopamine. The nucleus accumbens sits in a part of the brain responsible for organizing thoughts and emotions. It is often called the reward center of the brain.

The brain's reward for anything pleasurable is dopamine, said Dr. Nora D. Volkow, director of the National Institute of Drug Abuse, one of the National Institutes of Health.

"We do lots of things for dopamine," Volkow said. "We eat food for dopamine. We have sex for dopamine. Dopamine is the way nature motivates you to do things."

A combination of genetic factors that control the ebb and flow of dopamine in the brain also may determine whether a smoker becomes the one person in three who gets addicted to tobacco. . . .

A Crucial Enzyme

How long nicotine stays at high levels in an individual's blood is one of the key factors in determining who is likely to become a smoker, said Thomas C. Westfall, chairman of the Department of Pharmacological and Physiological Science at St. Louis University.

When a smoker lights up the first cigarette of the morning and takes a drag, nicotine rushes to the brain and bloodstream. In the body, a flood of adrenaline and noradrenaline constricts blood vessels and releases sugar into the blood, Westfall said. . . .

For most people the effects are short-lived, as enzymes in the liver quickly break down the nicotine. But some people have a genetic variation that decreases the amount of an enzyme called CYP2A6. The enzyme is responsible for breaking down nicotine, environmental toxins, including some found in tobacco smoke, and drugs such as the blood-thinner coumarin. People who have lower levels of the enzyme can't clear nicotine and may get nauseous, Westfall said. Those people tend not to become smokers, he said.

Howard McLeod of Washington University got interested in the enzyme because of studies that show differences in smoking habits and lung cancer rates between blacks and whites. He asked nonsmokers to chew nicotine gum for 30 minutes and then measured how quickly nicotine left the blood.

The African-Americans in the study tended to take longer to break down nicotine than their European-American counterparts, McLeod said. Genetic analysis revealed that about 5 percent of the white volunteers carried the genetic variant that lowers CYP2A6 activity, while 12 percent of the African-Americans had the variant, he said. A collaborator found that about 30 percent of Japanese people have the variation.

Those results could help explain some of the racial and ethnic differences in smoking habits, Bierut said. Black smokers tend to smoke fewer cigarettes than white smokers do. That could be because more blacks are unable to break down nicotine and need to smoke less to get the same amount of drug. . . .

Studies suggest that genetic differences could explain why African American smokers typically smoke fewer cigarettes than their Caucasian counterparts.

Because of a genetic variation in a nicotine-receptor gene, children with attention deficit disorder may have a higher risk of becoming addicted to smoking.

A Genetic Variation Leads to Increased Risk

A study of twins with Attention Deficit Disorder revealed that up to 70 percent of them are regular smokers, said Dr. Richard Todd, chief of child psychiatry at Washington University. The children often report that smoking helps them concentrate better, Todd said.

Children with Attention Deficit Hyperactivity Disorder, a syndrome often grouped with ADD but that Todd says has different genetic causes, were not as likely to smoke.

Todd and his colleagues examined the DNA of children with both disorders and found a genetic variation in a nicotine-receptor gene called CHRNA4. When nicotine binds to the receptors on brain cells, the cells release dopamine, which may aid concentration. The researchers are not yet sure how the variation affects the function of the nicotine-receptor. About 90 percent of the children with attention deficit carried the variant, but children with hyperactivity disorders had the variant no more often than would be expected by chance, Todd said.

The result could mean that drugs that alter the activity of some nicotine receptors could be effective treatments for Attention Deficit Disorder, and that children with the disorder should be warned of their increased risk of becoming addicted to smoking, Todd said. . . .

Just Beginning to Learn

Genetic studies of alcoholic families have revealed that some regions of the human genome may contain genes that contribute to addiction to alcohol and nicotine together, while other regions have genetic variations associated with alcoholism or smoking alone, said Bierut, the Washington University geneticist. Little is known about the genes located in those parts of the genome, she said. Most have no known function and their connection with nicotine or alcohol abuse is unclear.

Many genes may make small contributions to the process of nicotine or alcohol addiction, Bierut said. She and her colleagues are beginning a study of families who are heavy smokers to find some of the genetic factors that lead to nicotine addiction.

EVALUATING THE AUTHOR'S ARGUMENTS:

In the viewpoint you just read, author Tina Hesman describes several studies that appear to show a link between genetics and a person's predisposition to nicotine addiction. Considering what you have read on the subject, do you think a genetic explanation for nicotine addiction is plausible? Or are there other factors, such as advertising, economics, or social exposure, that you believe better explain why people smoke?

CHAPTER 3

Should Smoking Be Regulated?

Today, many public places prohibit indoor smoking.

Smoking Should Be Banned in Public Places

Arnold Baskies

"It begs reality that anyone could make an argument against an indoor smoking ban with a clear conscience."

In the following article, Arnold Baskies argues that banning smoking in public spaces is medically responsible and economically sound. He claims that tens of thousands of nonsmokers die each year from secondhand smoke, and so banning smoking from public spaces will save the lives of these innocent bystanders. It will also prevent workers in such establishments from being unfairly exposed to deadly smoke during their work shift. Furthermore, banning smoking in bars and restaurants will not have a negative economic impact on local industries, as the author claims the tobacco companies contend. Indeed, the author cites studies from several places in the United States where smoke-free restaurants and bars have continued to be economically viable despite bans on smoking. The author concludes that banning smoking in public places is a wise decision that saves the lives of nonsmokers and encourages smokers to quit a dangerous habit.

Dr. Arnold Baskies is chairman of the New Jersey Governor's Task Force on Cancer Prevention, Early Detection and Treatment, a panel comprised of doctors, nurses, researchers, and cancer survivors.

AS YOU READ, CONSIDER THE FOLLOWING QUESTIONS:
1. What do you think the author means when he accuses legislators of "running scared" from the tobacco industry?
2. According to the 2004 Zagat survey of New York City restaurants, how many more people have dined out since smoking was banned in bars and restaurants there?
3. According to the author, how many people are killed each year by secondhand smoke?

For years I've been waiting for the smoke to clear in New Jersey, and with the announcement [in September 2004] of a proposed smoking ban, that could be happening soon.

It is troubling to hear the public discussion on this vital public health issue reduced to a debate over the rights of smokers and nonsmokers, when I know this legislation is the difference between life and death for many. Countless studies have scientifically confirmed the devastating health effects of exposure to secondhand smoke. The evidence is so overwhelming, it begs reality that anyone could make an argument against an indoor smoking ban with a clear conscience.

[In September 2004] a new study revealed that the air in a smoky bar is nearly 20 times more carcinogenic than on I-95 at rush hour in Wilmington, Delaware.

As a physician and American Cancer Society volunteer, I am all too familiar with the devastating health effects of exposure to secondhand smoke. Secondhand smoke

FAST FACT

California, New York, Delaware, Maine, and Florida have bans on smoking in restaurants or bars. Smoking is also banned in either restaurants or bars in Tempe, AZ, Guadalupe, AZ, Cambridge, MA, Cape Cod, MA, Eugene, OR, Helena, MT, Tucson, AZ, Fort Wayne, IN, and several towns in West Virginia and Texas.

kills 65,000 people annually in this country, including 3,000 otherwise healthy nonsmokers through lung cancer.

To get a better sense of the death toll, imagine if the entire population of a city the size of Bayonne [New Jersey] were decimated this year. Sobering thought, isn't it?

For every seven smokers killed by tobacco use, one nonsmoker is also killed.

Putting Tobacco on the Defense

Of course, once debate starts on this legislation, no one will be up in arms about the tens of thousands of lives lost each year.

The tobacco industry will be blowing smoke about violations of smokers' rights. (Of course, this assumes that the right to smoke wherever one pleases is protected by law. It is not.)

Next, it will trot out the myth that a prohibition on smoking will bankrupt New Jersey's entire food and beverage industry. The contention that smoke-free establishments will lose business is just another Big Tobacco scare tactic.

Source: Bennett. © by Clay Bennett. Reproduced by permission.

The only negative economic effect of smoke-free-air laws and policies is on tobacco companies.

In fact, numerous scientific studies and economic analyses of sales tax receipts show that bar and restaurant business is not harmed by smoke-free policies.

California, the first state to institute a comprehensive smoking ban, has the longest track record in recording the ban's effect on business.

Since the statewide law went into effect in 1997, taxable sales receipts for bars and restaurants have consistently increased.

In addition, total employment at these establishments has increased every year.

Anti-Smoking Bill Will Not Hurt Business

New York implemented a sweeping ban [in 2003] that stirred up immense public debate. Vocal opponents cried that businesses, still suffering the economic effects of 9/11, would surely be forced to

The owner of this bar in Santa Monica, California, claims that his business increased dramatically after a statewide smoking ban took effect in 1998.

A group of smokers lights up outside a smoke-free restaurant in New York. Smoking has been banned in New York restaurants since 2003.

close their doors when smokers were forced to take their cigarettes outside.

Not true.

The 2004 Zagat New York City Restaurant Survey proves the smoking ban is not hurting business. The survey of nearly 30,000 restaurantgoers found 23 percent are eating out more often because of the smoke-free workplace law, while only 4 percent are eating out less.

Business owners in communities considering smoking bans are often the most outspoken opponents of such proposals. Very often, these same business owners turn into the most outspoken advocates for the measures once they take effect.

It's hard to argue against laws that have a positive impact on public health while adding to the bottom line.

It's About Saving Lives

However, it's not a question of the bottom line, or of someone's perceived right to smoke wherever they please. It's about saving lives, and the legislation introduced by [New Jersey State] Sen. John Adler (D-Camden) and Assemblywoman Loretta Weinberg (D-Bergen) recognizes that.

A statewide smoking ban will save millions of workers in our state from facing deadly conditions as the price for holding down a job. Workers who smoke also will find themselves in environments more supportive of their attempts to quit.

Smoking is no longer an acceptable public activity. More than 80 percent of the population says as much, by not choosing to smoke. It's time our legislators stop running scared from the tobacco industry and take measures to improve the health of New Jersey citizens. It's a move that will indeed leave a legacy.

EVALUATING THE AUTHORS' ARGUMENTS:

In the viewpoint you just read, author Arnold Baskies argues in favor of legislation that would ban smoking in public spaces. In the following viewpoint, author Arthur E. Foulkes argues against such legislation. After reading both articles, which argument do you find more persuasive, and why? Cite examples from the text in your answer.

Banning Smoking in Public Places Violates Individual Rights

Arthur E. Foulkes

"Most of us don't like breathing other people's smoke, but it is more an annoyance than an immediate threat to our lives."

Arthur E. Foulkes is a freelance writer. His work has appeared in the journal *Ideas on Liberty,* from which this viewpoint was taken. In the following viewpoint, Foulkes argues that smoking should not be banned in public places because it would negatively impact businesses and curb individual rights. He points out that if secondhand smoke is banned because it is considered an air pollutant, then there would be nothing to stop the prohibition of other activities that pollute the air, such as boating or riding in cars. Similarly, if it is determined that smoking should be banned in restaurants to protect children from being exposed to smoke, then smoking should, in theory, also be banned in private cars and homes, which the author suggests would be an absurd breach of liberty. The author also claims that antismoking bans would force businesses to bear excessive financial and political costs. The author concludes that it is not the government's responsibility to interfere in the economic or personal business of its citizenry, and therefore antismoking bans should be rejected.

AS YOU READ, CONSIDER THE FOLLOWING QUESTIONS:
1. According to the author, what does watching too much television or eating too much fast food have to do with exposure to secondhand smoke?
2. What does the use of the word *aggregated* mean in the context of the article?
3. According to the article, what were the findings of the National Opinion Research Center?

The war on smoking is proceeding with rapid progress. Antismoking activists are successfully fighting for smoking bans in restaurants, bars, bowling alleys, and other places open to the public. California and Delaware have banned smoking in virtually all restaurants and bars. Smoking is prohibited in restaurants in Maine, and voters in Florida recently approved a constitutional amendment that will do likewise. . . .

Smoke-Free Advocates Have Not Thought Things Through

Why all the bans? Advocates say they are protecting either children or workers (or both) from secondhand smoke, also known as environmental tobacco smoke (ETS). The Environmental Protection Agency (EPA) considers ETS to be a Category A carcinogen—meaning it is a substance known to cause cancer in humans. A federal judge later overturned the EPA's finding, noting the agency "adjusted established procedures and scientific norms" to reach its conclusion. . . .

Even if the EPA is right and ETS is harmful, does this justify government's telling property owners they can't allow smoking on their premises? According to smoke-free advocates, the answer is an unadulterated *yes.* New York Mayor Michael Bloomberg, who favors banning smoking in New York City bars, restaurants, and even outdoor cafes, puts the case this way: "Common sense and common decency demand . . . the need to breathe clean air is more important than the license to pollute it." (Does this mean we should also ban all other "non-essential" activities that pollute, such as pleasure boating, family vacations, and motorcycle rides?)

Bloomberg is an example of a full-bodied smoke-free advocate. This type wants government to protect workers by banning smoking in all workplaces, including bars. A more "mild" variety of smoke-free advocate only wants to protect children by banning smoking in restaurants, bowling alleys, and other places accessible to kids. Of course, some "milds" hope to extend restaurant bans to bars next. The chief executive of the American Cancer Society summed up the "full-bodied" view: "A bar is a workplace. You should not be allowed to smoke in a workplace."

The Myths of Protecting Children and Workers

The argument that children should not be exposed to secondhand smoke strikes a chord. After all, even libertarians believe government should protect citizens from harm inflicted by other citizens. If children are being abused when parents drag them into Denny's or some

Source: Hardin. © by Cartoonstock, Ltd. Reproduced by permission.

other restaurant where smoking is allowed, isn't it within the proper scope of government action to prevent such harm?

But if this is so, why stop at restaurants? Under this reasoning, smoking should be banned anywhere children are present, including private vehicles and homes. The smoke that kids of smokers breathe in a restaurant is negligible compared with what they get at home or on a drive. If ETS amounts to abuse, what possible difference does it make where the abuse takes place?

But parents permit or partake of lots of activities that might be detrimental to their children's health. Some allow their kids to eat lots of fast food or to watch too much television. Statisticians could quickly find correlations between these behaviors and bad health as well.

What about protecting workers? Many workplaces are unsafe or potentially unsafe. That creates a disincentive for many people to accept such jobs and allows perhaps less well-qualified and less particular workers to take the jobs. The element of danger or discomfort also forces employers to offer higher wages than otherwise. For those then willing to take the jobs, it means higher pay. By making work-

New York City mayor Michael Bloomberg (right) eats lunch in a smoke-free restaurant. The mayor endorsed a controversial plan to ban smoking in all public places in the city.

places smoke-free, some better-qualified workers will now be attracted to those jobs, driving the lesser-qualified workers into even less-desirable work—possibly at jobs with more immediate dangers—or out of work altogether.

Smoking Ban Studies Are Flawed

The war over smoking bans reached low ebb when the opposing sides started funding academic studies to argue that the bans are having either a positive or negative effect on the restaurant industry in smoke-free communities. Some restaurant trade groups sponsored studies showing a decrease in restaurant business after the smoking bans went into effect. . . .

Meanwhile, on the anti-smoking side, several studies (largely undertaken by smoke-free advocates, but never mind) have shown smoking bans have not harmed the restaurant industry. Some have even shown an *increase* in overall restaurant business. . . .

Does this mean economics supports the smoking bans? Not at all. All the studies supporting smoking bans are based on *aggregated* restaurant sales data; they look at the "restaurant industry" in the smoke-free communities. They largely ignore what might be happening under the surface to *individual* businesses and completely ignore the extent to which the bans further erode the essential concept of private property rights—the very linchpin of wealth creation in a market economy. . . .

Loss of Profit, Loss of Business

[Also,] for some restaurants or types of restaurants, the benefits of a smoke-free ordinance will outweigh the costs. For other restaurants and bars this will likely not be so. Blue-collar bars and restaurants, for example, may be especially hard hit, since, according to the National

This Maryland bar was forced to ban smoking in 2003. The owners complained the ban would cause them to lose business and was a violation of their patrons' rights.

Opinion Research Center, smoking is more common among blue-collar workers and people with lower incomes. Bars that cater to these customers may suffer a loss of business.

Moreover, where ordinances fall short of an outright ban, but require costly remodeling and nonsmoking sections, larger chain restaurants may be better able to cope than smaller competitors. For example, some ordinances require floor-to-ceiling dividers keeping bar areas separate from eating areas, or independent ventilation for smoking rooms. While overall restaurant business may increase, certain kinds of restaurants may suffer or go out of business. As usual, then, we see that government regulation of private business simply creates new winners and losers. It creates no new wealth, and, as we will see, actually squanders it. . . .

The more that government bodies usurp the ability of entrepreneurs to plan, the more they erode the role of entrepreneurship and deaden wealth creation [that is, hamper business owners' ability to make money]. Simultaneously, in such a system entrepreneurs begin spending time and resources not looking for new ways to satisfy consumers, but attempting to influence government, spending thousands or millions lobbying. In this way, wealth is actually squandered.

It's About Freedom

Most of us don't like breathing other people's smoke, but it is more an annoyance than an immediate threat to our lives. (Even directly smoking a cigarette does not instantly kill us like some exotic poison.) One smoke-free study found the number-one reason people avoid smoky restaurants is they don't like the lingering smell of cigarette smoke on their clothes and in their hair. My wife and I sometimes avoid places we know will be especially smoky. Other times we don't particularly care. It depends on our values at the moment. (She actually favors smoking bans, so I'm doing a little risk/benefit analysis[1] just by writing this.) Even the most strident smoke-free advocate may accept a table in a restaurant's smoking section if, for example, he is in a big hurry and wants the next available table. Just going to work or school each day involves risk/benefit analysis. It is simply a part of life.

Members of Congress, those people most eager to tell the rest of us how to live, allow individual members to decide the smoking policy in their own offices on Capitol Hill. Restaurant and bar owners should have the same freedom, even if large majorities favor a ban on smoking. Workers too should be free to work where they would like and make their own risk/benefit tradeoffs. And parents, not the government, should be responsible for their children's well-being. By usurping the parental role, governments not only seize authority over children, but also make children out of adults. This approach, in addition to being morally destructive, is bad economics as well—regardless of what the econometric analyses say.

EVALUATING THE AUTHOR'S ARGUMENTS:

In the viewpoint you just read, author Arthur E. Foulkes rejects the notion of government intervention in the economic and personal business of its citizenry. In your opinion, does banning smoking in public places constitute a breach of liberty? Why or why not? Explain your answer using evidence from the articles you have read on this topic.

1. Risk/benefit analysis is the comparison of the risk of a situation to what may be gained from it.

Tobacco Advertising Should Be Banned

Nigel Gray

"Complete bans on tobacco advertising work."

In the following viewpoint, author Nigel Gray argues in support of a ban on tobacco advertising. He claims that advertisements for tobacco products are powerful, persuasive, and omnipresent. He believes a ban on advertising would curb smoking levels and save people from becoming addicted to cigarettes. However, he concedes that an outright ban on advertising will be difficult to achieve, and so recommends a comprehensive program for how to fight the influence of tobacco products. He concludes that although the battle against the tobacco industry is bitter and difficult, the benefits of preventing smoking are worth it. Therefore, banning tobacco advertising should remain the long-term goal of the public health establishment.

As a consultant for the European Institute of Oncology, Nigel Gray works on cancer prevention and control.

Nigel Gray, "Tobacco Industry and EC Advertising Ban," *The Lancet,* vol. 359, April 13, 2002, p. 1,264. Copyright © 2002 by The Lancet, Ltd. Reproduced by permission of Elsevier.

AS YOU READ, CONSIDER THE FOLLOWING QUESTIONS:
  1. According to the author, what did Mark Neuman and his colleagues expose about the tobacco industry?
  2. What does the author consider to be "the ultimate advertisement"?
  3. What are three actions the author suggests should be part of the fight against tobacco?

I n [the April 13, 2002, edition of the] *Lancet,* [writer] Mark Neuman and colleagues analyse in detail the way in which the tobacco industry worked against an advertising ban within the European Community (EC). The revelations in this cautionary tale may startle public-health workers. Using documents from the tobacco industry brought into the open by court cases, Neuman and colleagues report on how the industry works and exemplify its comprehensive approach to achieving its market-expanding objectives—of which mortality expansion [that is, death of tobacco consumers] is a by-product.

American tobacco companies sponsor spectator events, such as this car race in Malaysia, to circumvent laws against tobacco advertising.

Advertising's Bitter Grip

The industry had lobbied at the highest political level in Europe to try to prevent the EC from passing a directive to ban tobacco advertising and sponsorship. . . . Neuman and colleagues show that the tobacco industry has attempted to use as part of its blocking strategies the principle of subsidiarity, in which the EC cannot over-rule individual member states. A watered-down directive, largely limited to cross-border activities, is now being discussed. It will always be dif-

Over 1 million Chinese die from smoking each year. To counter the problem, the Chinese government has begun to introduce antismoking ads.

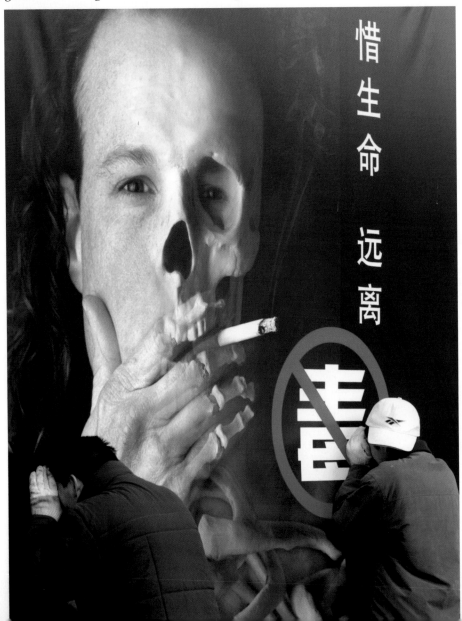

ficult to achieve public-health objectives in this environment and a total advertising ban probably lies beyond the EC's present powers.

Cross-border advertising on satellite television is potent and ubiquitous. In a single afternoon watching television in India I saw tobacco-industry sponsored: cricket from India, motor-car racing from Europe and Macau, motor-bike racing from Europe, golf from Indonesia, and soccer played before an empty stadium emblazoned with tobacco advertising (country unknown).

Complete bans on tobacco advertising work. Legislation providing such bans required a single act in Norway and Finland, but a 30-year battle in Australia (which is also a federation). However, no such ban is ever complete, because the ultimate advertisement still exists—a teenager offers a cigarette from an attractively branded packet to a friend. Because of skillful marketing, cigarettes still have a strong general appeal as a product, especially to young people. This is not to suggest that bans are unnecessary, merely that they are not enough.

We Need a Worldwide Ban on Tobacco Ads

A worldwide ban on advertising will probably require agreement between public-health professionals and the tobacco industry. Such an agreement may necessitate finding an acceptable way in which the industry can be allowed to make a profit in a declining market. The idea that the public-health establishment should sit down and settle an agreement with the tobacco industry rendered that establishment divided and indecisive in the USA, and is likely to do so again. Nevertheless that experience demonstrated that duress can bring the industry to the bargaining table in a realistic frame of mind. . . .

Nevertheless the public-health establishment needs to decide what it wants and then to fight for it. The fight does start with the best possible ban on advertising. The fight includes expensive counter-advertising funded by a tobacco tax and continued indefinitely (each year pours a new crop of teenagers into the vulnerable age groups). A stronger approach

WHERE TOBACCO ADVERTISING SHOULD BE LIMITED TO.

Source: Ramsey. © 1996 by Copley News Service. Reproduced by permission.

to cessation is essential, based on free access to nicotine-replacement products, better support from doctors, and better products—perhaps even addictive on their own. Restrictions on smoking in public places also work. These approaches deal with initiation and maintenance of smoking but harm-reduction must not be neglected. Regulations and regulators are needed in all countries to set upper limits for cigarette emissions, as are laboratories and experts to control and monitor the process. This process can only start with political decisions, which will not come unless driven by public-health forces.

Problems Must Be Addressed

There are some imponderables here. Can the public-health establishment face up to negotiating with the tobacco industry? To the continued existence of a profitable tobacco industry? To the possibility of recreational clean nicotine? To attempts to reduce the addictiveness of cigarettes by reducing their nicotine content? To deciding what limits should be set for carcinogens and toxins? Can they even decide who should lead them? All that in the face of the industry's delaying tactics and marketing skills which have worked globally—and Neuman and colleagues reveal that that influence continues.

The problems outlined here are not an excuse for doing nothing, and battles are not lost until they are fought. Doing whatever is possible remains today's policy. Massachusetts, California, Australia, and Sweden all have unusually low smoking rates of 20% or less, yet none have perfect programmes. In the longer-term, those involved in tobacco control need to agree on policy and leadership and to work coherently at a global level.

EVALUATING THE AUTHOR'S ARGUMENTS:

In the viewpoint you just read, Nigel Gray believes it is the government's responsibility to protect people from smoking. Opponents of this view argue that the government's decision to interfere in the private decisions of citizens constitutes a breach of liberty. Considering what you know on this issue, how involved do you think a government should be in regulating smoking among its citizens? Explain your answer using evidence from the articles you have read.

VIEWPOINT 4

Tobacco Advertising Should Not Be Banned

Hugh High

"Evidence contradicts the surmise that people . . . begin consuming tobacco products as a result of advertising."

In the following viewpoint Hugh High argues against attempts to ban the advertising of tobacco products. He notes that efforts to ban tobacco advertisements are based on the assumption that such advertising causes increased smoking. However, he contends that this assumption is flawed; rather than promote smoking, advertising merely entices existing smokers to switch brands. High also rejects calls to limit tobacco advertising as a means to protect children from the harms of tobacco. Young people are induced to smoke not by advertising, High insists, but due to the smoking habits of their family members and peers. Hugh High is an economist and lawyer who was previously the director of the finance department at the University of Cape Town in South Africa.

AS YOU READ, CONSIDER THE FOLLOWING QUESTIONS:
1. What is the difference between the advertising of new products and mature products, according to the author?

Hugh High, *Does Advertising Increase Smoking? Economics, Free Speech, and Advertising Bans.* London: Institute of Economic Affairs, 1999. Copyright © 1999 by the Institute of Economic Affairs. Reproduced by permission.

2. How many British smokers switch brands each year, as reported by High?
3. Why would a ban on tobacco advertising inhibit the development of more healthy tobacco products, in the author's opinion?

The conventional rationale of the right of government to restrict tobacco advertising is protection of the health of the citizenry and particularly of younger members of society who are alleged to be both particularly deserving of protection and particularly susceptible to the lure of commercial tobacco advertising. . . .

The Goal of Tobacco Advertising

Virtually all companies, including monopolies, advertise. Much of this advertising is not intended to increase the number of people who use the 'product category'. Rather, advertising is employed for a variety of reasons depending on whether the product is in a 'new product' category or a 'mature' one and on whether the product category is in competition with other categories.

With new product categories such as cellular telephones, videocassette recorders or personal computers, advertising aims to inform people about their general attributes and benefits, rather than to promote a particular *brand*. As consumer awareness of the product category expands, advertising faces a mature market. Examples of mature markets include petrol [gasoline], toothpaste, soap, laundry detergent, telephones, and television sets. There is a large literature which demonstrates that in such mature markets advertising is not significantly related to aggregate product demand but aims to raise demand for the advertised brand. This fact was even acknowledged, as recently as 1994, by the US Institute of Medicine.

Nonetheless, it has been argued by some, including the American Food and Drug Administration (FDA), that cigarettes are not a mature market because the tobacco industry must continue to advertise so as to 'lure' young people into the market. This reflects a total failure to understand what is meant by a mature product.

The simple fact is that every mature market—whether automobiles, houses, television sets, cigarettes, washing machines, and so on—has first-time buyers who have never previously purchased the product. Manufacturers of cigarettes are no more dependent on new buyers than are other manufacturers of mature products. It is entirely rational for manufacturers of goods in mature markets to advertise in order to increase or maintain their existing market share. In the UK, total annual sales of cigarettes are over £12 billion so that gaining an additional 1 per cent share means gaining sales of well over £100 million.

Ad Bans Stifle Knowledge

The importance of maintaining market share is especially acute in the British tobacco industry which is faced by evidence that more than 1 in 3 smokers switch brands every year. Advertising, then, is a highly effective way to ensure that keen competition exists in the tobacco market-place which bans and restrictions on advertising can only stifle, thereby entrenching established firms.

In conclusion, it should be emphasised that were advertising of tobacco products to be banned, it would be more difficult for consumers to acquire knowledge of new products, including cigarettes with lower tar and nicotine and so-called 'smokeless' cigarettes. It would therefore inhibit the development of such products, as well as making it more difficult for new entrants with 'specialised' products to enter the market. . . .

The Problems with Ad Bans

A rationale commonly advanced for regulating tobacco products is that smoking among the young is increased by advertising. While our concern here is not with trends in youth smoking, it is instructive to note that, as Peter van Doren has recently demonstrated, short-term trends in behaviour often mask longer term trends and give the appearance that youth smoking rates have changed. This illustrates the per-

A billboard along a Dallas highway comments on the smoking restrictions imposed in the late 1990s. In 1999 the major U.S. tobacco companies agreed to remove all advertising from billboards across the nation.

ils of focusing attention on short-run periods. When viewed over longer periods, 'the data demonstrates that the trend in youth smoking is rather benign' and that 'the alarmist view of smoking behaviour by minors is not consistent with the data over the last twenty years'.

Despite this important finding, it is frequently argued by advocates of advertising bans that even if advertising has little or no effect on consumption by adults, children are rather more impressionable

Source: Asay. © 1999 by Creators Syndicate, Inc. Reproduced by permission.

and thus more likely to be affected by advertising. There are a number of problems with this argument. Advertising bans designed to protect children also deprive adults of the right to consume/enjoy commercial speech in the form of advertising which in turn precludes them from making informed decisions on tobacco products. Further, advertising restrictions make it difficult for new firms to enter the market, and thus deprive consumers of new and possibly more beneficial products, including lower tar/nicotine products. Moreover, a ban on advertising removes the incentive for established producers to develop such products as a response to competitive pressures, and thus discourages innovation in the market for tobacco products.

Leaving these and related arguments aside, there are a number of good reasons against advertising restrictions designed to protect children. An immense amount of evidence contradicts the surmise that people generally, and children particularly, begin consuming tobacco products as a result of advertising. Research demonstrates that the most important determinants of initiation into smoking are: (a) whether members of the family smoke, and (b) whether peers smoke.

Awareness Is Not Consumption

Advocates of restrictions are fond of pointing to studies showing that children are aware of various tobacco adverts, most prominently 'Joe Camel' and 'the Marlboro man'. Yet awareness hardly implies that the viewer will consume the product advertised, which would mean that advertisers have an automatic sales machine. The idea that consumers generally, and children in particular, are 'puppets of Madison Avenue' has no foundation in fact, despite the populist tirade of authors, such as John Kenneth Galbraith and Vance Packard. Serious academics in marketing and economics give such arguments little or no credence.

. . . There are various reasons why some people are more aware of particular advertisements than others; the existence of 'selective perception' is well known in both psychology and marketing. . . . There is ample evidence that children who are aware of advertising: (a) typically have family members who smoke, and (b) typically assert that, while aware of advertising, they have no intention of beginning to smoke. Perception is not consumption.

Without prejudging the health/medical arguments on smoking, tobacco companies are universally in the forefront of wishing to stop cigarettes being sold illegally to minors. It is at least likely that a ban would lead to a weakening of the effort to enforce the law against under-age smoking.

EVALUATING THE AUTHORS' ARGUMENTS:

Nigel Gray and Hugh High have different opinions on the potency of tobacco advertising. Nigel Gray believes it is a powerful and influential force, while Hugh High considers its effect on people to be minimal. After reading both viewpoints, what is your opinion on the efficacy of tobacco advertising? Do you think that curbing advertising would have an effect on the number of people who smoke? Why or why not?

GLOSSARY

Big Tobacco: Refers to the network of tobacco manufacturers, distributors, and marketers. The term *Big Tobacco* was introduced in the 1990s and includes tobacco manufacturers such as RJ Reynolds, Philip Morris, Brown and Williamson, and Lorrilard.

carcinogen: Any substance that causes cancer.

cessation: Refers to quitting smoking or using smokeless tobacco. There are a variety of programs and products that can help with tobacco cessation, including a wide range of nicotine gums and patches.

dopamine: A neurotransmitter present in regions of the brain that regulate emotion, motivation, and feelings of pleasure.

emphysema: A lung disease in which the tissue in the lungs deteriorates, resulting in difficult breathing and shortness of breath. Smoking and exposure to secondhand smoke frequently result in emphysema.

environmental tobacco smoke (ETS): Also referred to as passive or secondhand smoke. It is the smoke that is in the air after a smoker exhales. Secondhand smoke has been shown to be dangerous to people who are in the vicinity of people who are smoking.

filter: A fibrous material bound to the end of a cigarette to filter out tar that is found in cigarette smoke.

nicotine: A colorless, poisonous organic compound derived from the tobacco plant. It is the substance in cigarettes to which smokers become addicted.

1998 Master Settlement Agreement (MSA): A watershed agreement in which the tobacco industry agreed to pay $206 billion in damages to forty-six states for the medical costs incurred by smokers. The MSA also required tobacco companies to finance a $1.5 billion antismoking campaign and to cease refuting evidence that smoking is harmful to human health. The MSA further banned tobacco advertising on billboards and in certain types of magazines, and prohibited tobacco advertisements from using cartoons or other images that might appeal to children.

FACTS ABOUT SMOKING

Editor's Note: These facts can be used in reports or papers to reinforce or add credibility when making important points or claims.

Smoking in the United States

According to several Morbidity and Mortality Reports compiled by the Centers for Disease Control and Prevention (CDC):

- Cigarette smoking has been identified as the most important source of preventable morbidity and premature mortality in the United States and the world.
- Smoking-related diseases cause an estimated 440,000 American deaths each year.
- Smoking costs the United States over $150 billion annually in health care costs.
- In 2002, an estimated 45.8 million, or 22.5 percent, of American adults were smokers.
- Smoking rates of Americans are highest among Native Americans/Alaskan Natives, at 40.8 percent. Hispanics and Asians and Pacific Islanders have the lowest rates of smoking, at 16.7 percent and 13.3 percent, respectively.
- A 2004 study by the CDC's National Center for Chronic Disease Prevention and Health Promotion found that cigarette smoke contains over 4,800 chemicals, 69 of which are known to cause cancer.

Smoking and Women

According to the U.S. surgeon general:

- Although the number of male smokers still exceeds the number of female smokers, each year the gap between the two groups grows smaller. In 2002, 20 percent of all American women smoked. Health experts consider the growing rate of smoking among American women to be reaching critical proportions.
- Women account for 39 percent of all smoking deaths.
- Since 1980, 3 million women have died of smoking-related diseases.

According to the American Lung Association:

- In 1987 lung cancer surpassed breast cancer as the leading cause of cancer deaths among women in the United States.

- Cigarette smoking kills approximately 178,000 women in the United States every year.
- Women smokers who succumb to a smoking-related disease lose on average 14.5 years of potential life.
- Women who smoke have an increased risk for developing cancers of the mouth, pharynx, larynx, esophagus, pancreas, kidney, bladder, and uterine cervix.
- Teenage girls often start smoking to avoid gaining weight and to iden-tify themselves as independent and glamorous. Cigarette advertising suggests that smoking suppresses one's appetite.
- In 2003, 21.9 percent of high school girls were smokers.

The Effects of Smoking on Pregnancy and Infancy

According to the American Lung Association:

- In 2002, 11.4 percent of mothers smoked during pregnancy.
- Cigarette smoking during pregnancy can cause many health problems for both mother and child, such as pregnancy complications, prema-ture birth, low birth-weight infants, stillbirth, and infant death. Smoking during pregnancy accounts for 20 to 30 percent of low birth-weight babies, up to 14 percent of preterm deliveries, and 10 percent of all infant deaths.
- Mothers who smoke can pass nicotine to their children through breast milk.
- Cigarette smoking prevents as much as 25 percent of oxygen from reaching the placenta, the organ that nourishes a fetus.
- Infants born to mothers who smoke are more likely to develop colds, bronchitis, and other respiratory diseases such as asthma. The odds of developing asthma are twice as high among children whose mothers smoke more than ten cigarettes a day.

Smoking and Teenagers

- According to the results of a National Youth Tobacco Survey, one-third of all adult smokers had their first cigarette by the age of four-teen. Ninety percent of all smokers begin before age twenty-one.
- The Substance Abuse and Mental Health Services Administration has found that 6,000 children under the age of eighteen smoke their first cigarette on any given day. The administration estimates that nearly 2,000 of them become regular smokers, resulting in 757,000 new ado-lescent smokers every year.

According to the Centers for Disease Control and Prevention:

- In 2003, 22 percent of all high school students smoked.
- In 2002, 10 percent of all middle school students smoked.
- In 2002, 6.1 percent of all high school students and 3.7 percent of middle school students used smokeless tobacco.

According to the American Legacy Foundation:

- People who begin smoking in adolescence are more likely to develop a severe addiction to nicotine than those who start at a later age. Of adolescents who have smoked at least one hundred cigarettes in their lifetime, most report they are unable to quit.
- Adolescents who have two parents who smoke are more than twice as likely as youth without smoking parents to become smokers.
- A 2001 survey found that 69.4 percent of teenage smokers reported never being asked for proof of age when buying cigarettes in a store. The same survey found that 62.4 percent were allowed to buy cigarettes even when the retailer was aware they were under eighteen.

Secondhand Smoke

- The EPA has classified secondhand smoke as a carcinogen since 1992. The agency estimates approximately three thousand people die annually in the U.S. from exposure to secondhand smoke.
- More than 10 million young people aged twelve to eighteen live in a household with at least one smoker.
- A study published in the *New England Journal of Medicine* found that nonsmokers exposed to secondhand smoke were 25 percent more likely to have coronary heart diseases compared to nonsmokers not exposed to smoke.
- According to a 2002 survey undertaken by *Archives of Pediatric Adolescent Medicine,* 21 million, or 35 percent, of American children live in homes where residents or visitors smoke in the home on a regular basis.
- According to the EPA, approximately 50–75 percent of children in the United States have detectable levels of cotinine, the breakdown product of nicotine, in their blood.
- According to a 2001 study released by the *Journal of Occupational and Environmental Medicine,* on average about 70 percent of the U.S. workforce works under a smoke-free policy. The levels ranged from 83.9 percent in Utah to 48.7 percent in Nevada.

ORGANIZATONS TO CONTACT

The editors have compiled the following list of organizations concerned with the issues debated in this book. The descriptions are derived from materials provided by the organizations. All have publications or information available for interested readers. The list was compiled on the date of publication of the present volume; the information provided here may change. Be aware that many organizations take several weeks or longer to respond to inquiries, so allow as much time as possible.

Action on Smoking and Health (ASH)
2013 H St. NW, Washington, DC 20006
(202) 659-4310
Web site: www.ash.org

Action on Smoking and Health promotes the rights of nonsmokers and works to protect them from the harms of smoking. ASH worked to eliminate tobacco ads from radio and television and to ban smoking in airplanes, buses, and many public places. The organization publishes the bimonthly newsletter *ASH Smoking and Health Review* and fact sheets on a variety of topics, including teen smoking, passive smoking, and nicotine addiction.

American Cancer Society
1599 Clifton Rd. NE, Atlanta, GA 30329
(800) ACS-2345 (227-2345)
Web site: www.cancer.org

The American Cancer Society is one of the primary organizations in the United States devoted to educating the public about cancer and to funding cancer research. The society spends a great deal of its resources on educating the public about the dangers of smoking and on lobbying for anti-smoking legislation. The American Cancer Society makes available hundreds of publications, ranging from reports and surveys to position papers.

American Council on Science and Health (ACSH)
1995 Broadway, 2nd Fl., New York, NY 10023-5860
(212) 362-7044

fax: (212) 362-4919
e-mail: acsh@acsh.org
Web site: www.acsh.org

ACSH is a consumer education group concerned with issues related to food, nutrition, chemicals, pharmaceuticals, lifestyle, the environment, and health. It publishes the quarterly newsletter *Priorities* as well as the booklets *The Tobacco Industry's Use of Nicotine as a Drug* and *Marketing Cigarettes to Kids.*

American Lung Association (ALA)
1740 Broadway, New York, NY 10019-4374
(212) 315-8700
fax: (212) 265-5642
e-mail: info@lungusa.org
Web site: www.lungusa.org

Founded in 1904, the American Lung Association is the oldest voluntary health agency in the United States. It is dedicated to the prevention, cure, and control of all types of lung disease, including asthma, emphysema, tuberculosis, and lung cancer. ALA's mission is to prevent lung disease and to promote lung health.

American Medical Association (AMA)
515 N. State St., Chicago, IL 60610
(312) 464-5000
Web site: www.ama-assn.org

The AMA is the largest professional association for medical doctors. It helps set standards for medical education and practices and is a powerful lobby in Washington for physicians' interests. It publishes the weekly *JAMA,* the *Journal of the American Medical Association.*

Americans for Nonsmokers' Rights
2530 San Pablo Ave., Suite J, Berkeley, CA 94702
(510) 841-3032
fax: (510) 841-3071
e-mail: anr@no-smoke.org
Web site: www.no-smoke.org

Americans for Nonsmokers' Rights seeks to protect the rights of nonsmokers in the workplace and other public settings. It works with the American

Nonsmokers' Rights Foundation, which promotes smoking prevention, nonsmokers' rights, and public education about involuntary smoking. The organization publishes the quarterly newsletter *ANR Update,* the book *Clearing the Air,* and the guidebook *How to Butt In: Teens Take Action.*

American Smokers Alliance (ASA)
PO Box 189, Bellvue, CO 80512
fax: (970) 493-4253
e-mail: derf@smokers.org
Web site: www.smokers.org

The American Smokers Alliance is a nonprofit organization of volunteers who believe that nonsmokers and smokers have equal rights. ASA strives to unify existing smokers' rights efforts, combat antitobacco legislation, fight discrimination against smokers in the workplace, and encourage individuals to become involved in local smokers' rights movements. It publishes articles and news bulletins, including "Smokers Have Reduced Risks of Alzheimer's and Parkinson's Disease" and "Lung Cancer Can Be Eliminated!"

Canadian Council for Tobacco Control (CCTC)
75 Albert St., Suite 508, Ottawa, ON K1P 5E7 Canada
(800) 267-5234
(613) 567-3050
fax: (613) 567-5695
e-mail: info-services@cctc.ca
Web site: www.cctc.ca

The CCTC works to ensure a healthier society, free from addiction and involuntary exposure to tobacco products. It promotes a comprehensive tobacco control program involving educational, social, fiscal, and legislative interventions. It publishes several fact sheets, including *Promoting a Lethal Product* and *The Ban on Smoking on School Property: Successes and Challenges.*

Cato Institute
1000 Massachusetts Ave. NW, Washington, DC 20001
(202) 842-0200
Web site: www.cato.org

The institute is a libertarian public policy research foundation dedicated to limiting the control of government and protecting individual liberty.

Its quarterly magazine *Regulation* has published articles and letters questioning the accuracy of EPA studies on the dangers of secondhand smoke. The *Cato Journal* is published by the institute three times a year and the Cato Policy Analysis occasional papers are published periodically.

Children Opposed to Smoking Tobacco (COST)
Mary Volz School, 509 W. Third Ave., Runnemede, NJ 08078
e-mail: costkids@costkids.org
Web site: www.costkids.org

COST was founded in 1996 by a group of middle school students committed to keeping tobacco products out of the hands of children. Much of the organization's efforts are spent fighting the tobacco industry's advertising campaigns directed at children and teenagers. Articles, such as "Environmental Tobacco Smoke" and "What You Can Do," are available on its Web site.

Coalition on Smoking OR Health
1150 Connecticut Ave. NW, Suite 820, Washington, DC 20036
(202) 452-1184

Formed by the American Lung Association, the American Heart Association, and the American Cancer Society, the coalition has worked to revise warning labels on tobacco products and to ban smoking in public places. It seeks to restrict advertising of tobacco products, to increase tobacco taxes, to regulate tobacco products, and to prohibit youths' access to tobacco products. It publishes the report *Tobacco Use: An American Crisis,* the briefing kits Leveling the Playing Field and Saving Lives and Raising Revenue, as well as fact sheets and several annual publications.

Competitive Enterprise Institute (CEI)
1001 Connecticut Ave. NW, Suite 1250, Washington, DC 20036
(202) 331-1010
fax: (202) 331-0640
e-mail: info@cei.org
Web site: www.cei.org

The institute is a pro–free market public interest group involved in a wide range of issues, including tobacco. CEI questions the validity and accuracy of Environmental Protection Agency studies that report the dangers of secondhand smoke. Its publications include books, monographs, and policy studies, and the monthly newsletter *CEI Update.*

Environmental Protection Agency (EPA)
Indoor Air Quality Information Clearinghouse
PO Box 37133, Washington, DC 20013-7133
(800) 438-4318
(703) 356-4020
fax: (703) 356-5386
e-mail: iaqinfo@aol.com
Web site: www.epa.gov/iaq

The EPA is the agency of the U.S. government that coordinates actions designed to protect the environment. It promotes indoor air quality standards that reduce the dangers of secondhand smoke. The EPA publishes and distributes reports such as *Respiratory Health Effects of Passive Smoking: Lung Cancer and Other Disorders* and *What You Can Do About Secondhand Smoke as Parents, Decisionmakers, and Building Occupants.*

Fight Ordinances & Restrictions to Control & Eliminate Smoking (FORCES)
PO Box 14347, San Francisco, CA 94114-0347
(415) 675-0157
e-mail: info@forces.org
Web site: www.forces.org

FORCES fights against smoking ordinances and restrictions designed to eventually eliminate smoking, and it works to increase public awareness of smoking-related legislation. It opposes any state or local ordinance it feels is not fair to those who choose to smoke. Although FORCES does not advocate smoking, it asserts that an individual has the right to choose to smoke and that smokers should be accommodated where and when possible. FORCES publishes *Tobacco Weekly* as well as many articles.

Food and Drug Administration (FDA)
5600 Fishers Ln., Rockville, MD 20857
(888) INFO-FDA (888-463-6332)
Web site: www.fda.gov

An agency of the U.S. government charged with protecting the health of the public against impure and unsafe foods, drugs, cosmetics, and other potential hazards, the FDA has sought the regulation of nicotine as a drug and has investigated manipulation of nicotine levels in cigarettes by the tobacco industry. It provides copies of congressional testimony given in the debate over regulation of nicotine.

Foundation for Economic Education
30 S. Broadway, Irvington-on-Hudson, NY 10533
(914) 591-7230
fax: (914) 591-8910
e-mail: fee@fee.org
Web site: www.fee.org

The foundation promotes private property rights, the free market economic system, and limited government. Its monthly journal, the *Freeman,* has published articles opposing regulation of the tobacco industry.

Group Against Smoking Pollution (GASP)
PO Box 632, College Park, MD 20741-0632
(301) 459-4791

Consisting of nonsmokers adversely affected by tobacco smoke, GASP works to promote the rights of nonsmokers, to educate the public about the problems of secondhand smoke, and to encourage the regulation of smoking in public places. The organization provides information and referral services and distributes educational materials, buttons, posters, and bumper stickers. GASP publishes booklets and pamphlets such as *The Nonsmokers' Bill of Rights* and *The Nonsmokers' Liberation Guide.*

KidsHealth.org
Nemours Foundation Center for Children's Health Media
1600 Rockland Rd., Wilmington, DE 19803
(302) 651-4000
fax: (302) 651-4077
e-mail: info@KidsHealth.org
Web site: www.KidsHealth.org

The mission of KidsHealth.org is to help families make informed decisions about children's health by creating the highest quality health media. It utilizes cutting-edge technology and a wealth of trusted medical resources to provide the best in pediatric health information. Its teen section covers a wide variety of issues, including teen smoking. *How to Raise Non-Smoking Kids* and *Smoking: Cutting Through the Hype* are two of its numerous publications.

Libertarian Party
1528 Pennsylvania Ave. SE, Washington, DC 20003
Web site: www.lp.org

The goal of this political party is to ensure respect for individual rights. It opposes regulation of smoking. The party publishes the bimonthly *Libertarian Party News* and periodic Issue Papers.

National Center for Tobacco-Free Kids/Campaign for Tobacco-Free Kids
1707 L St. NW, Suite 800, Washington, DC 20036
(800) 284-KIDS (284-5437)
e-mail: info@tobaccofreekids.org
Web site: www.tobaccofreekids.org

The National Center for Tobacco-Free Kids/Campaign for Tobacco-Free Kids is the largest private initiative ever launched to protect children from tobacco addiction. The center works in partnership with the American Cancer Society, American Heart Association, American Medical Association, the National PTA and over one hundred other health, civic, corporate, youth, and religious organizations. Among the center's publications are press releases, reports, and fact sheets, including *Tobacco Use Among Youth, Tobacco Marketing to Kids,* and *Smokeless (Spit) Tobacco and Kids.*

Reason Foundation
3415 S. Sepulveda Blvd., Suite 400, Los Angeles, CA 90034
(310) 391-2245
Web site: www.reason.org

The Reason Foundation is a libertarian research and education foundation that works to promote free markets and limited government. It publishes the monthly *Reason* magazine, which occasionally contains articles opposing the regulation of smoking.

SmokeFree Educational Services, Inc.
375 South End Ave., Suite 32F, New York, NY 10280
(212) 912-0960
Web site: www.smokefreeair.org

This organization works to educate youth on the relationship between smoking and health. It publishes the quarterly newsletter *SmokeFree Air* and the book *Kids Say Don't Smoke* and distributes posters, stickers, and videotapes.

Smoker's Rights Alliance
20 E. Main St., Suite 710, Mesa, AZ 85201
(602) 461-8882

The alliance challenges antismoking legislation and discrimination against smokers. It believes that disputes about smoking should be settled by individuals, not by government regulations prohibiting smoking. It publishes *Smoke Signals* quarterly.

Smoking Policy Institute
218 Broadway, Seattle, WA 98102
(206) 324-4444

The institute assists companies in solving the problems created by smoking at work. It helps companies develop and implement customized smoking control policies through information packages and consulting services. The institute maintains a resource center of articles and statistics on smoking, and it publishes booklets and videotapes on workplace smoking.

The Tobacco Institute
1875 I St. NW, Washington, DC 20006
Web site: www.tobaccoinstitute.com

The institute is the primary national lobbying organization for the tobacco industry. The institute argues that the dangers of smoking have not been proven and opposes regulation of tobacco. It provides the public with general information on smoking issues.

Tobacco Merchants Association of the United States
PO Box 8019, Princeton, NJ 08543-8019
(609) 275-4900
fax: (609) 275-8379
e-mail: tma@tma.org
Web site: www.tma.org

The association represents manufacturers of tobacco products; tobacco leaf dealers, suppliers, and distributors; and others related to the tobacco industry. It tracks statistics on the sale and distribution of tobacco and informs its members of this information through the following periodicals: the weekly newsletters *Executive Summary, World Alert,* and *Tobacco Weekly;* the biweekly Leaf Bulletin and Legislative Bulletin; the monthly *Trademark Report* and *Tobacco Barometer: Smoking, Chewing and Snuff;* and the quarterly newsletter *Issues Monitor.* The association has a reference library, offers online services, and provides economic, statistical, media-tracking, legislative, and regulatory information.

Tobacco Products Liability Project (TPLP)
Tobacco Control Resource Center
Northeastern University School of Law
400 Huntington Ave., Boston, MA 02115-5098
(617) 373-2026
fax: (617) 373-3672
e-mail: tobacco@bigfoot.com

Founded in 1984 by doctors, academics, and attorneys, TPLP studies, encourages, and coordinates product liability suits in order to publicize the effects of smoking on health. It publishes the monthly newsletter *Tobacco on Trial.*

Books

John Harvey and M.D. Kellogg, *Tobaccoism or How Tobacco Kills.* Kita, MT: Kessinger, 2003. Discusses how tobacco has long been known to doctors, chemists, and pharmacists as a very deadly plant.

Arlene B. Hirschfelder, *Kick Butts.* Lanham, MD: Scarecrow, 2001. Provides information on how tobacco companies advertise to the public and influence legislation. Discusses various successful programs schoolchildren have initiated for smoke-free environments. Excellent for young readers.

Jason Hughes, *Learning to Smoke: Tobacco Use in the West.* Chicago: University of Chicago Press, 2003. Examines the diverse sociological and cultural processes that have compelled people to smoke since the practice was first introduced to the West during the sixteenth century.

Leonard A. Jason et al., *Preventing Youth Access to Tobacco.* Binghamton, NY: Haworth Press, 2003. The author discusses how policy makers have sought more effective ways to use public policy to reduce tobacco use and to promote smoking cessation.

David Kessler, *A Question of Intent: A Great American Battle with a Deadly Industry.* New York: Public Affairs, 2002. The author of this book was head of the Food and Drug Administration for seven years under Presidents George H.W. Bush and Bill Clinton.

Lynn T. Kozlowski, *Cigarettes, Nicotine, and Health.* Thousand Oaks, CA: Sage, 2001. Considers both the biological and psychosocial influences on smoking behavior.

Judith Mackay, ed., *The Tobacco Atlas.* Geneva, Switzerland: World Health Organization, 2002. Includes full-color world maps and graphics that reveal similarities and differences between countries on the history of tobacco, different types of tobacco use, prevalence and consumption, youth smoking, the economics of tobacco, farming, and manufacturing, smuggling, and many other topics. An excellent resource for reports.

Laury Oaks, *Smoking and Pregnancy: The Politics of Fetal Protection.* New Brunswick, NJ: Rutgers University Press, 2001. This book argues that health educators should consider the daily lives of women and their socioeconomic status to understand why some women choose to smoke during pregnancy.

Tara Parker-Pope, *Cigarettes: Anatomy of an Industry from Seed to Smoke.* New York: New Press, 2001. This book, written by a *Wall Street Journal* reporter, looks at the history of cigarettes and addresses why people start smoking, why they continue, and what it costs.

Robert L. Rabin, ed., *Regulating Tobacco.* New York: Oxford University Press, 2001. This collection of essays explores specific strategies that have been used to influence tobacco use.

W. Kip Viscusi, *Smoke-Filled Rooms: A Postmortem on the Tobacco Deal.* Chicago: University of Chicago Press, 2002. This book, written by a Harvard law professor and tobacco industry expert witness, argues that the 1998 tobacco settlement was politically driven and that the tobacco companies made a mistake in settling with the states.

Mark Wolfson, *The Fight Against Big Tobacco: The Movement, the State, and the Public's Health.* Berlin: Aldine de Gruyter, 2001. Examines how the tobacco control movement has become a significant force in shaping contemporary public policy, social norms, and the habits of millions of Americans.

Periodicals

Catherine Arnst, "The Skinny on Teen Smoking," *Business Week,* December 2, 2002.

Diana M. Bonta, "Tobacco Tax Kills 2 Birds with 1 Stone," *Los Angeles Daily News,* July 12, 2002.

Eric Boyd, "The Risks of Smoking Are Greatly Exaggerated," *Kitchener-Waterloo Record* (Ontario), November 20, 2002.

Joseph H. Brown, "Smoke Screens and Health Statistics," *Tampa Tribune,* October 6, 2002.

Center for Communications, Health, and the Environment, "Women, Girls, and Tobacco: An Appeal for Global Action," July 6, 2002. www.ceche.org.

Centers for Disease Control and Prevention, "Youth Tobacco Use and Exposure Is a Global Problem," August 28, 2002. www.cdc.gov.

Kathie Cheney, "Smoking Ban Can Be a Lifesaver," *Atlanta Journal-Constitution,* April 2, 2004.

Marlene Cimons, "Tobacco's Toll on Women," *Los Angeles Times,* March 28, 2001.

Economist, "Smoke and Fire; Genetics and Smoking," November 27, 2004.

Thomas R. Eddlem, "Individual Rights Going Up in Smoke," *New American,* August 26, 2002.

Josh Fischman, "Dangers of Secondhand Smoke—and Secondhand Research," *U.S. News & World Report,* May 21, 2003.

Colorado Springs Gazette, "Duty-Free, Sort Of; as Tobacco Taxes Rise, Black Market in Cigarettes Thrives," July 20, 2002.

Pradeep P. Gidwani, "Television Viewing and Initiation of Smoking Among Youth," *Pediatrics,* September 2002.

Wayne Grytting, "Philip Morris Sees the Light," *Z Magazine,* October 2001.

Philip Hensher, "Society Is Losing a Civilizing Habit," *Independent* (London), August 24, 2001.

Janice M. Horowitz, "Sweet as Candy, Deadly as Cigarettes: Teens Are Flocking to a Hip Form of Smokes. There Are Hidden Dangers," *Time,* December 16, 2002.

Derrick Z. Jackson, "How Big Tobacco Is Rising from the Ashes," *Boston Globe,* May 2, 2003.

Holman W. Jenkins Jr., "Sue the Ones You Love," *Wall Street Journal,* September 29, 2004.

Sharon Johnson, "Cigarette Break: No Longer Cool, Smokers Find Themselves Out in the Cold," *New York Times,* November 18, 2003.

Kathiann M. Kowalski, "How Tobacco Ads Target Teens," *Current Health 2,* April/May 2002.

Michael D. LaFaive, "The Unintended Consequences of Cigarette Tax Hikes," Mackinac Center for Public Policy, December 13, 2002. www.mackinac.org.

Kelle Louaillier, "Big Tobacco Undermines the American Way," *People's Weekly World,* June 30, 2001.

Shawn Macomber, "Relighting the Tobacco Wars," *American Spectator,* July/August 2004.

Tom Majeski, "Teenage Smoking Drops 11% in 2 Years," *Pioneer Press,* September 20, 2002.

Peter J. Mazzone and Alejandro C. Arroliga, "How Many Ways Can We Say That Cigarette Smoking Is Bad for You?" *Chest,* December 2004.

David Nelson, "Clearing Air over Secondhand Smoke," *Rocky Mountain News,* July 19, 2002.

People's Weekly World, "Quitting Smoking Boosts Girls' Self-Esteem," June 23, 2001.

Peter Pringle, "Why They Keep on Lying," Index on Censorship, April 2004.

Shari Roan, "'Safer' Cigarettes Appeal to Some, but Appall Others," *Los Angeles Times,* June 10, 2002.

Ted Roberts, "I Never Dream of Nicotine," *Ideas on Liberty,* May 2003.

Gilbert L. Ross, "Big Tobacco's No. 1 Lie Is That 'Everyone Knows,'" *Los Angeles Times,* August 2, 2001.

Paul R. Sanberg, "Surprise: Nicotine May Actually Be Beneficial Sometimes," *American Medical News,* March 20, 2000.

Terrence Scanlon, "A Better Alternative to the 'Quit or Die' Approach to Tobacco," Townhall.com, September 27, 2003.

David Simpson and Stan Shatenstein, "Pushing and Peddling," *New Internationalist,* July 2004.

Tobacco Retailer, "Study: Tobacco Ads Still Targeting Children," October 2001.

Susan Turney, "Raise Tobacco Tax; Help State, Smokers," *Madison (WI) Capital Times,* February 2, 2005.

Marjorie Williams, "Smoking Is Killing American Women," Washington Post Weekly Edition, April 16–22, 2001.

Zoe Williams, "Fag End of Fashion," *New Statesman (1996),* April 19, 2004.

Jack Wheeler, "Nightmare of Crack Nicotine; the Alternative to Cigarettes Is Much Worse," *Washington Times,* August 29, 2002.

Sidney Zion, "The Big Lie of Secondhand Smoke," *San Francisco Examiner,* November 29, 2002.

Web Sites

N.Y.C. CLASH—Citizens Lobbying Against Smoker Harassment (www.nycclash.com). This pro-smoker's rights Web site focuses on the debate over smoking in New York City. It contains a wealth of pro-smoking, antitaxation, and antismoking ban viewpoints collected from editorials, periodicals, journals, song lyrics, and blog entries.

Scene Smoking (www.scenesmoking.org). This Web site, run by the American Lung Association, keeps a current list of movies and ranks them according to their tobacco content. Contains interesting information about smoking and international film industries around the world, and offers readers a chance to review movies for the site.

Smoke Free Movies (www.smokefreemovies.ucsf.edu). Smoke Free Movies is a project of Stanton A. Glantz, a professor of medicine at the University of California, San Francisco. Smoke Free Movies aims to reduce the number of movies that feature smoking or portray the habit in a positive light, and to end brand advertising in movies.

The Truth.com (www.thetruth.com). The Truth.com is funded by the American Legacy Foundation, a public health organization created in 1998 as a result of the Master Settlement Agreement. The Truth.com is known for conducting its antismoking campaign with an edgy, in-your-face style meant to appeal to teenagers. The Web site contains facts about smoking, games, poster downloads, and event information.

INDEX

PICTURE CREDITS

ABOUT THE EDITOR

Lauri S. Friedman earned her bachelor's degree in religion and political science from Vassar College. Much of her studies there focused on political Islam, and she produced a thesis on the Islamic Revolution in Iran titled *Neither West, Nor East, But Islam.* She also holds a preparatory degree in flute performance from the Manhattan School of Music, and is pursuing a master's degree in history at San Diego State University. She has edited over ten books for Greenhaven Press, including *At Issue: What Motivates Suicide Bombers?, At Issue: How Should the United States Treat Prisoners in the War on Terror?,* and *Introducing Issues with Opposing Viewpoints: Terrorism.* She currently lives near the beach in San Diego with her yellow lab, Trucker.